ISBN   978-0-9964150-2-6

Captain Fielding, Master Mariner

A Convict Voyage to Australia

Warren Dent

Captain Fielding, Master Mariner

A Convict Voyage to Australia

Table of Contents

Part One – England 1810

Chapter 1

Standing just inside the front door, the Captain pulled on his heavy overcoat and elegant top hat. Through the small fan-shaped leaded window above, he could tell that a light mist was present outside, a harbinger of the usual winter evening fog. He added gloves to his ensemble, but decided the umbrella could stay in its stand. The lamplighter hadn't yet made his rounds, and more often than not these days he never appeared. Since Parliament was planning on introducing gas lighting for the streets of London by 1812, less than two years hence, many lamplighters were already seeking other employment.

"Will you be home at the usual hour, Captain?" Mrs. Hutchinson inquired. She knew the answer because the Captain's routine never varied, but habit still made her ask. As the Captain's housekeeper for the last three years, she knew more about many of the man's customs than he did. This was part of the relationship that they both implicitly treasured – a redundant inquiry of respect and caring that, by its presence, reassured each other that everything was normal and as it should be. Once in a while there would be a little extra, or something new, in their exchanges. Such as yesterday when she surprised him at morning tea with a small birthday cake she'd made for his 47th. He had smiled and chuckled and had been clearly pleased. Mrs. Hutchinson savored his positive reaction.

"Ten past five, not a moment beyond, Mrs. Hutchinson," the Captain responded, and with that he stepped out into the deepening gloom. No matter which of the three possible routes he selected, the Rose and Thorn pub was a brisk twelve minute or so walk away. The longest route by a smidgeon of time skirted the river in part. An unusual inner voice made him hesitate momentarily and directed him to make the river walk tonight's choice. A Captain in the Royal Navy, he loved being near, on, or in the water. The Thames was tame compared to the mighty oceans of the world he had experienced, but he found its tidal-dependent, reversible flow a constant reminder of the power of nature.

His new boots made a soft crunching sound on the cobblestones of the first alley, pleasing him with the steady rhythm that arose. Head down, concentrating on the regularity of the beat, he missed the cry at first. But, coming out of his reverie, he heard a sharp, pleading female voice yelling "Help me, help!"

Immediately concerned, he sprinted to the end of the alley where he stopped, unsure whether to turn left or right. Ordinarily he would have turned left and headed along the river bank, and on to the pub beyond. To the right where the river made a major turn, he knew there were a series of warehouses, closed now at 7 pm, but with numerous entrances, loading docks, and assembly yards where dirty deeds could take place fairly well-hidden.

He hurried in that direction, listening attentively for further cries, and was frustrated at hearing none. From a narrow lane beside one of the buildings a dark-coloured cat suddenly rushed out, surprising him with its shrill hissing, and nearly tripping him. It was his best clue, and he turned into the path, slowing his gait. No direct light penetrated down through the fog, the area tightly hemmed in by the tall wooden commercial structures. A faint moon-glow reflecting off the river from behind was the only light he had to guide him. Something caught his eye to the side and he turned to find a pair of boots and trousered legs stretched out from under an overturned cart, the pockets pulled inside out. With determined effort he quietly lifted the edge of the cart but put it down quickly. A young man lay motionless in a pool of blood surrounding his head, a knife protruding sickeningly from the side of his neck. A thought flashed through the Captain's mind wondering why the knife was left in place – perhaps indicating the killer had been disturbed in his act, and was possibly still very close by.

A second thought made him stop and retrieve the knife so that he now had a weapon. In daylight he wouldn't have considered it, because his huge size at six feet six inches tall and seventeen stone, about 240 pounds, in weight, he was a formidable opponent in any face-to-face combative situation. Coupled with his champion pugilist background, he was more than a match for most men and there was little that scared him. The weapon would certainly signal his seriousness and preparation, but could also be used as a distraction, or, if necessary, thrown into the back of a fleeing coward.

A scratching sound from up ahead stopped him. Rats, another cat, or a woman in distress trying to provide a weak signal? He stooped now and moved slowly forward up the incline, one deliberate step after another. A guttural noise that was part shriek, and a slapping sound from just ahead to the left brought him upright and he ran forward. In a few long strides he came across a man holding a woman on the landing of a short flight of steps leading up to double doors in a ramshackle storage building. A dim light reflected off the recessed doors allowing him to see that the woman's dress lay askew across the landing and her petticoat was drawn up to her knees, but that a large piece had been torn off and stuffed in her mouth. Her arms extended behind her back, presumably tied together at the elbows or wrists, and the man was pulling hard on her hair with one hand forcing her head down onto a thick wooden block. His other hand explored high up under the remnants of her petticoat. She was kicking ferociously and squirming from side to side, but he was leaning over close to her face, clearly threatening her with looks and whispered words.

The woman's eyes moved to the side as she noticed the Captain. Observing her glance, the murderer sensed a new presence, and turned to find a veritable giant rushing at him. The Captain didn't utter a word, simply threw the knife down, and wrapped two massive arms around the assailant's neck. The man hurriedly brought his arms up to try and release the ferocious grip now holding him, letting the woman's head loll backwards, free at last. The Captain dragged the attacker down the steps, then lifted him up a foot in the air, and slammed his head against a six inch thick metal stanchion to which another cart was tied.

The man was clad in tattered old clothes, stained and ill-fitting, but must have had a constitution of iron that belied his looks, for he shook his head, swore vehemently, and lashed out at the Captain, who stepped back and levelled a devastating kick to the man's crotch with his new boots. As the swine doubled over, the Captain balled his right fist and slammed it into the man's throat.

Most men would have succumbed under such treatment, but surprisingly, this chap raised himself up coughing and gasping, and instinctively tried to flee. His intention was transparent and the Captain was ready; he tripped the man easily as he tried to run away. Another crotch kick followed by one to the side of the head and the assailant lay motionless, now thoroughly defeated. The Captain rushed to the woman and pulled the cloth from her mouth and used it to tie the chap's hands behind his back. He then picked up the knife and cut through the rope tying the woman's arms as she sputtered over and over, "Thank you sir, thank you, thank you. You saved my life. He killed my husband and clearly would have killed me too, after he was done with me. Thank you, thank you!"

The Captain knelt beside her, helping her to sit upright, and gently spoke: "I regret I couldn't save your husband, ma'am. I was too late, and I'm terribly sorry for your loss. I need to make sure this ruffian won't move while I go fetch a constable, so if you'll turn away for a moment I'll get to work. I promise he won't hurt you anymore." So saying, he moved back, reached down and ripped the man's shirt off, then sat him against the stanchion and used part of the rope to tie his hands behind it. He fashioned the remainder of the rope into a noose which he pulled tightly around the man's neck, tying the other end to the heavy cart, facing it downhill. The Captain judged him to be about thirty years old. It was somewhat hard to tell, as his face was grotesque, with unsightly boils and growths across his cheeks, and large warts on his nose. Definitely one of London's less pretty people.

Small specks of foam were at the edge of his mouth and several teeth were missing, most of those remaining being yellow with brown stains. He was breathing hard from the beating he'd received. His ugliness could only have added to the woman's terrified reactions to his presence and intentions. The Captain stripped the man of his britches, throwing them in the cart, causing unmistakable embarrassment. As the chap started to curse and complain at this act, the Captain punched him hard under the chin, silencing him totally.

The woman was now crying inconsolably, sitting on the top step with her clothes gathered back around her. Her bodice had also been torn apart and she couldn't hide the nasty bruises and welts around her breasts that were now vaguely apparent in the gloomy light. The Captain took off his coat and wrapped it around her shoulders, covering her up as best he could. He placed his hat over her roughed-up hair, hoping to add warmth to her scalp. She looked to be a similar age to her assailant, maybe a few years younger, although in the gloom he wasn't really sure. He could distinguish that a little color was creeping back into her cheeks but shock was still apparent. He was reluctant to leave her with the perpetrator and her dead husband nearby, but had little choice. He attempted to provide reassurance. "Lady, he is tied up as best I can. I'll leave the knife with you while I go find an officer. If he tries anything don't hesitate to use it." At this suggestion her eyes opened wide, her face screwed up, and she shook her head, a tremor of terror passing through her body. Clearly the notion was completely repugnant even after the terrible drama she'd suffered through.

"Just hurry back please sir. Hurry. Thank you." And with that the Captain raced off to the Rose and Thorn where he knew he'd find Constable Hinman in his favorite spot. The publican, Ben, greeted him warmly. "Captain Fielding, we've been wondering where you were." "Sorry Ben, we have a problem. Simon, you need to come with me. Do you know if any of your comrades on the force are nearby? We have a murder and a young woman nearly raped down at the warehouses. I've got the murderer tied up. Got there a bit late I'm afraid, but now you need to get involved and take over."

Once outside, Hinman blew his whistle repeatedly as he followed the Captain back to the crime scene. He pointed to the dead husband but ran by. The woman was lying sobbing on the landing, staring with hatred at the assassin. Shock was still in play, and the Captain sat and wrapped his arms around her, offering heartfelt sympathy and comfort. A fellow constable soon turned up, and after the Captain repeated what he knew, he left things in the hands of the officers and slowly returned to the pub, his mind wondering at the senselessness of the crime. He had asked Simon to bring his coat and hat around when it was appropriate, but to let the woman keep them for as long as they were useful.

Back at the pub, the crowd of regulars clamoured for information, and he reluctantly told the sad tale a couple of times. The patrons, most of whom knew him well, regaled him as a hero, a label he rejected, saying anyone else would have done the same. From the description he provided, it turned out that the couple had actually been at the pub earlier, having had a meal that they washed down with ale. They were visiting the city from Birmingham and had decided to end their day with a stroll along the river. Ordinarily no one thought twice about doing the same sort of sightseeing, it being a relatively peaceful part of town east of the city proper with only trivial crime, usually amounting to nothing more than the stealing of men's handkerchiefs or wallets.

Everyone was shocked to hear of a murder and wondered what the police would learn about the villain. In the western suburbs, where the massive influx of job-seeking dispossessed rural families was overwhelming the supply of jobs, serious and violent crime was running rampant. Was it now spreading eastward? The Captain and others shuddered at the thought.

Despite his late arrival, the Captain ordered his usual dinner, but had one less drink than normal. As much as he tried to minimize them, the cheers and handshakes he experienced for his actions warmed his soul. It felt good to help others and to be recognized by his close friends. But it didn't mean he would bask in any glory. Being a man used to strict discipline, routine, and behavior, he finished his after-dinner drinks at 9:50 pm and headed home. He deliberately chose one of the alternative routes in order to be well away from the tragic scene.

He felt for the poor visiting woman. What a terrible introduction to the big city. What would her life be like now? How dependent had she been on her husband? Were there children involved? Were there relatives back home she could lean on for support? Did she possess an inner strength that would allow her to carry on? He hoped so.

Life definitely was not fair. An innocent evening stroll had unexpectedly become an instrument of an abruptly more-restricted life. A meaningless death, and terror that the survivor of the attack would never forget. Anger flooded the Captain's breast.

He wondered about the murderer as well. What had driven him to such a violent, depraved action? Had he simply wanted money and accosted the young couple with a request for a handout, but had been refused? Was he so desperately in need that he decided to kill in order to take the man's wallet? His countenance suggested he was a man who only appeared at night, possibly begging on the streets or searching rubbish piles and the river for food or pawnable items. There was a tinge of pity in the Captain's heart for the life the man had been reduced to pursue, but, even so, it was still no reason for killing. Would he cough up his tale to the constabulary or hold his voice until a lawyer was supplied?

The Captain knew he'd eventually hear from Simon on another evening.

At 10:02 pm precisely Mrs. Hutchinson added water to the kettle and started it heating on the stove. She reached up and got down the Captain's favorite cup and saucer from the cupboard and stood by the hall entrance to the kitchen waiting his return. At the sound of his key in the lock, she brushed the curls back from her forehead and straightened out her apron. She liked to look nice for her landlord and rescuer. She had a natural sunny disposition and a twinkle in her eyes that reflected her joy of living. Without the Captain's intervention and aid after her husband and sister died, her only alternative eventually would have been life in a parish home or, worse, life on the streets. She was enormously grateful, and happy to look after the Captain per his wishes. As he entered the doorway she moved forward to help him remove his coat , then stopped short and exclaimed "Captain, what happened to your overcoat and top hat?"

"I'll be happy to tell you over that cuppa the kettle is whistling about, Mrs. Hutchinson. It's been quite an eventful evening."

As was their custom, they sat on opposite sides of the old oak kitchen table. She filled the teapot and let the brew stew for a bit before pouring a strong serving into his cup that already had a teaspoon of sugar and a little milk in it.

"Ah, exactly what I needed after a colder walk home than usual. Thank you Mrs. Hutchinson, now let me tell you my tale."

It wasn't the first such tale he had brought home with him, for the Captain's life had always been quite colourful. He was on active commission in the Royal Navy, anxiously waiting his next assignment. In fact he had only been home ten days after several months at sea, captaining a freighter on several trips to and from the American colonies. Mrs. Hutchinson looked after his place during his extended absences, keeping it clean and tidy and handling the few bills that inevitably arrived while he was gone. It was a modern, narrow, two storey house, squeezed between taller homes that were owned by a merchant on one side and a doctor on the other. Located on a quiet street in a fashionable suburb that bordered the Thames, it was relatively close to several shops and not far from the center of the city. Captain Fielding had no siblings and both parents had passed on a few years ago allowing him to make the purchase with his Navy earnings and family inheritance.

Many years before, he had graduated from the Royal Naval Academy in Portsmouth. Initially he'd been a bit of an embarrassment, for his record in his first years there was not stellar. The problem was that he was very bright, his father a renowned Naval Admiral and his mother a teacher. His incidental schooling at home had prepared him well to follow in his father's footsteps, and the exercises and lessons at the Academy were simply not challenging enough. Boredom turned him surly, and he threw his weight and strength around easily, picking on his classmates and running afoul of some of his instructors.

Finally, with startling insight, an older administrative official suggested he take out his boredom and aggression in the boxing ring. The young man took to the sport immediately, and as his body toned and his strength and boxing prowess progressed, his academic malaise dropped away and he ended up at the top of his class, to his father's chest-swelling pride. Simultaneously, he was recognized as the Naval boxing champ, yet, for a sport known for its roughness, he never succumbed to negative personality traits or behavior, always thanking his opponents, never bragging, and withholding blows when an opponent was clearly done for. As a result he became known as the 'gentleman boxer.'

His at-sea assignments were passed with flying colors, and he climbed through the ranks much faster than the average Academy graduate. His proudest accomplishment was captaining one of the 74-gun ships in Lord Nelson's column of the armada which defeated Napoleon's fleet off the coast of Spain at Cape Trafalgar in October 1805. His ship was badly damaged but it had been one of those that helped create a decisive victory, breaking the back of the French and Spanish resistance. He lost nearly thirty men when enemy cannon found their mark, but he commandeered the ship safely to Gibraltar and eventually limped back to Portsmouth to the grand welcome and national celebration. The Battle of Trafalgar was a turning point in the Napoleonic wars. While Vice Admiral Nelson died from a sniper's shot, and 450 other men were killed and over 1200 wounded, the country rejoiced in the victory. The Captain was glad to have served and wore his decorative medal with pride.

In September 1807 he participated in the revengeful but successful outcome of the Battle of Copenhagen. His arrival back home, by contrast, was devastating. He learned that his parents had died in a terrible fire that had consumed several connected houses on their street. He had loved his mother and father deeply for, in his view, their unselfish guidance and support had been major factors responsible for his success in life. To him it was ironic that while he was absent fighting for his country against a dangerous enemy, putting his ship and men at great risk, his parents died helplessly at home, victims of irresponsible drunken domestic neighbors. Victory at sea seemed meaningless compared to the personal loss at home.

The emotional impact of the tragedy on the Captain's demeanor was a major surprise to his fellow officers and comrades. His enthusiasm for battle was no longer driven by the old passion and fervor, and his private dream to rise to the rank of admiral like his father fell away. The usual spring in his step was no longer evident, although his love of the sea was undaunted. Accordingly, he asked for relief from any specific warship captaincy, and was reassigned to captaining merchant ships plying the Atlantic between England and America. Naval engagements due to national pride were still in vogue in the Napoleonic wars and most merchantmen ships carried cannon, as skirmishes between French, Spanish and British fleets still took place. In recognition of the possible risks, naval captains with war-time experience were deployed to guide the freighters through potentially perilous seas. Captain Fielding actually welcomed his new assignment, and never regretted his decision to leave direct war-time command.

The change meant moving to London, which provided additional relief in a way, as he was no longer obliged to remain the city where his parents had died. He had asked Mrs. Hutchinson if she'd be interested in being his housekeeper in the big city. It was a life-changing opportunity for the widow, one which she accepted most thankfully.

Since the move three years ago, her sense of indebtedness had progressed to one of wife-like commitment and devotion, although she carefully repressed any thought of desire for a potential wedded relationship. She was essentially content to serve and provide as needed. Always cognizant of the Captain's generosity, she gave thanks each night in bedside prayer, and in deep internal sighs whenever the front door opened and her man stepped safely across the threshold.

She worried that one day he wouldn't come home.

Chapter 2

Anne Charlotte Rollings was born in the coastal town of Plymouth in June 1763. Her father was a poor but happy fisherman, adored by her mother. Anne had a sister Eliza Mary who was older by only eighteen months, so the pair grew up together and were inseparable as playmates. Anne's blonde curls and pleasant round face contrasted with Eliza's straight hair and angular looks. Where Anne was chubby, Eliza was thin, so that strangers questioned whether they really had come from the same pod. Both were average students, leaving school early to become maids in the houses of local upper class gentry, in order to bring in extra family income.

At age twenty, Anne fell in love with a neighbor who lived a block away. William Hutchinson was a handsome lad with a perpetual sly grin that could turn into a captivating smile at the smallest provocation. He was a labourer on the docks of Devonport, the Navy's major dockyard, where he helped load and unload supplies and perform light maintenance functions on the ships of the Navy's fleet. He and Anne were married in a small local chapel, and a year later Anne produced a son they named Edward James after her father. William never knew his father, and his mother had no real love for him. Over the years there'd been a number of men in and out of the tiny flat where his mother took in washing and ironing to help make ends meet. His positive outlook belied the less than savory background of his upbringing.

Traditionally, sisters married in the order they were born, but Eliza seemed to have no interest in men, being very self-reliant and happy to be unencumbered with a mate. She harbored no ill will that Anne married first. Perhaps she had a sixth sense about marriage, for she was certainly wary of William, seeing something that didn't ring true behind his public face. She suggested to her sister more than once that she should be hesitant about any full-blown trust of him. She pointed out that his mother's life-style was not a healthy one and that in the long term its influence might eventually come to light in unacceptable behavior. Anne simply never understood her sister's concern and her stand-offish relationship with Anne's husband, and a small wedge entered their relationship.

Unfortunately, Eliza's foresight was to prove prescient, as over the years William came to doubt his worthiness in the presence of smart young sailors, and started to drink excessively.

By age ten Edward was witness to his mother being beaten on a semi-regular basis. Like many abused wives, Anne thought that with patience, love, and sympathy, she could cure her husband, but it was not to be. Her son often tried to physically intervene, but five years on, after being repeatedly thrashed, and unable to offset his father's violence, he simply ran away. The last Anne heard of him, he was working in the Hemerdon tin mine seven miles to the northeast in Plympton, sleeping in a makeshift home with a number of other waifs of similar age. She was brokenhearted at the loss of her boy, for in her mind he was the main reason for continuing to stay with her husband.

Life-sparing relief came in an unexpected way when one morning three years later William staggered to work, well and truly drunk as usual, and tripped over a bollard on the dock. Devonport was an innovative facility, being the first of its type to use stone rather than wood in the construction of its piers. In falling down, William cut his head deeply on the stone base, and as he clutched his face to stem the flow of blood, he rolled dangerously close to the wharf edge. He stretched out to grab hold, but his bloody hands slipped and he tumbled over the side, his body bouncing painfully on the stepped stones twelve feet down to the water. His drunken yells were heard widely and men rushed to rescue him, in vain. He was still alive when dragged from the water, but with a broken back, half drowned from his fill of liquor and oily water, and still bleeding from the nasty gash across his forehead, he expired before the doctor arrived thirty minutes later.

It was December 1802, and the bitter winter wind off the Atlantic wrapped Anne in misery as she stared at William's cheap pine coffin. No tears were shed at his funeral, and as much as Anne wondered if her son might show up, he never appeared, and she bore her mild sense of grief at his absence alone.

Being good-hearted, sister Eliza, still a spinster, invited Anne to come live with her in Portsmouth, Hampshire, one hundred and seventy miles to the east. As it was another naval town, the transition was far less difficult than a move to an inland country town might have been. In any event Anne had little choice, and she was incredibly thankful for her sister's love and offer. Not once did Eliza say "I told you so," although Anne recognized that she certainly deserved to be reminded of Eliza's earlier insight.

"Anne, I can't imagine going through what you have these past sixteen years. And I'm sure I could never understand the grief you feel in losing both a son and husband. It will take ages to heal, to bring back those chubby cheeks and curls that I envied as a youngster. You are welcome to share this abode as long as necessary. There is no obligation whatsoever, and I will not pry into your past life. You may share whatever you wish and I will listen. But I want you to be active and not to sit around moping, as I think activity will hasten your return to what must seem like an elusive normal existence."

It took the better part of a year for Anne's cheeks to fill out and her hair to retrieve much of its childhood's luster. She diligently walked around the town for exercise every day, attended church regularly and volunteered to read to students at the church school. She willingly helped with household duties in Eliza's home, and when Eliza indicated that a vacancy was about to occur in the office where she worked, she anxiously applied for the position.

It was time to be a real person again.

The sisters became an inspiration to their fellow workers at the Naval Academy with their positive attitude and willingness to take on any task requested of them. With the announcement of Nelson's victory at Trafalgar late in 1805 they spearheaded the clerical staff's efforts at organizing the massive celebration planned for the armada's return to port.

At the actual event there was tinge of sadness present in several of the speeches, for many men had died in the service of their country. The minute of silence accorded their memory seemed totally inadequate to Anne, and she headed outside the mammoth pavilion to get a breath of fresh air. The deaths of so many brave young men brought back sad memories of the loss of her son. He would be twenty one years old now, the same age as many of the conscripts who had fought and died for their country. She'd not dwelled on her son's fate in many years but she now found herself sobbing for both him and herself. The child she had loved unconditionally had left home irrevocably. She couldn't and wouldn't blame him, but the tears flowed freely in recognition of the permanence of his departure.

A gentle hand on her shoulder made her turn, a handkerchief in one hand dabbing at her eyes. A gigantic man in full Captain's uniform, his face creased in sympathy, stood towering over her. "My lady, I am distressed by your condition. May I be of assistance? I'm Captain Fielding of the Nelson armada."

"You are so kind, Sir, thank you. I am sad at the cost of victory in terms of soldiers' lives, although I am fortunate my son was not among them. I apologize for my indiscretion at a time of celebration."

"Your sentiments do you proud, my lady. There are probably many mothers who feel similarly. Is your son here as well?"

"No, sir, it is six years since he left for the tin mines back in Devon. I don't know why I am telling you this, but he was beaten by his father and escaped further punishment by running away. I understand and forgive him for that, but I miss him. His father, my husband, died three years ago."

Anne paused as she reined in her emotions. "I guess I should not be so selfish, as there are many mothers present who have lost their sons forever. I still have hope that one day I may find mine again."

The Captain read between the lines easily. "I wish you good luck in your quest, Madam. You clearly have suffered much but I admire your respect and concern for others. May I have the honor of knowing your name?"

With a slight bow of her head Anne introduced herself. "Mrs. Hutchinson at your service, Sir. Congratulations on a wonderful victory. May it help to put an end to these incessant wars."

Captain Fielding stood erect, a smile spreading across his craggy good looks, and saluted. "May you be blessed in your endeavours, Mrs. Hutchinson. I wish you God's full protection. It was a pleasure meeting you."

With that he turned and disappeared back inside the pavilion. Anne was left open mouthed, re-living the conversation with this stranger. Little did she know how it was to change her life forever.

Chapter 3

The rain drummed heavily on the roof and against the small kitchen window in the front of the house. It had been pouring ever since the small hours of the morning, but the sun was now adding a little light behind the heavy clouds. She'd seen the first errand boys of the day running swiftly past the overflowing street gutters to fetch horses and carriages for the transport work ahead.   The Captain was either sleeping in, or had already risen and was at his desk adding more notes to his memoirs.

Mrs. Hutchinson climbed the wooden stairs in her stockinged feet for the third time, not wanting to wake the man if indeed he was still in bed. The rain was so noisy on the roof tiles that it was unlikely she'd be heard even with regular boots on. Back downstairs, she started heating water and filling the pails, anticipating that the Captain would want his usual bath when he finally did arise.

Unsurprisingly, five minutes later he entered the kitchen with a bright "Good morning, Mrs. Hutchinson. I see you are getting my bath water ready. That's splendid, thank you." He had on his woolen pajamas and warm slippers with a faded red dressing gown tied around his middle that was too short for his giant frame.   "I do wish you'd let me buy you a better fitting gown, Captain," Mrs. Hutchinson said for the umpteenth time. "It's not right that a gentleman like you shouldn't have the best clothes."

"You do mother me so, Mrs. Hutchinson. I love this old sack. It has protected me for years, but I daresay some down-and-out street person may find it comforting as well. As soon as I come back from my next assignment I'll have you shop for a new one. Does that please you?"

Anne's eyes lit up and she beamed from ear to ear. "It will be my pleasure, Captain. Now will you help me carry these pails upstairs to the bathtub, please?" She tried to always address the Captain with a tone of deference even though they were the same age, having been born in 1763, albeit months apart in towns nearly 200 miles distant from each other. Over the last three years in particular since they had been together, Anne had worked hard at becoming a robust, happy woman, content with the lot that God had accorded to her. The Captain had played a pivotal role in her destiny.

When he had returned from the Copenhagen battles in late 1807, and found his parents had died, the Captain was naturally depressed. He remembered meeting a woman at the celebration of the Trafalgar victory two years earlier, and her words about loss of family resonated in his memory. He had forgotten her name, but with determined effort he sought her out, thinking that there was more he could learn from her in his own world of grief. The woman was Anne Hutchinson, and her poignant story had haunted him ever since their earlier meeting. There quickly developed a wonderful mutual chemistry between the two of them that warmed their hearts and souls. It was a bold suggestion to ask her to be his housekeeper in London, and he was thrilled when she accepted.

Anne's sister had died of consumption in 1806, and she had some money put away from the sale of the little house Eliza had owned. The Captain advised Anne on investments and had helped her savings grow nicely. As such she had no wish to forego the arrangement she had with him, although there were occasions when she wished for a little more intimacy in their relationship.

She left the warm water beside the tub and closed the door for the Captain's privacy. There was a small knot-hole between two of the vertical oak slats in the door through which she was able to peer and admire the Captain's physique. He had a barrel chest, tight abdomen, muscular arms and legs, and an attractively sized man-piece. She'd looked in several occasions before and always felt guilty afterwards, although sometimes a sweet sensation ran through her body as a result. "Still a few sensitive female feelings left," she told herself whenever it happened.

Returning to the kitchen, she decided to make bread. She loved cooking, and had found that while in many facets the Captain was a creature of habit, he was quite open to experimenting with different food dishes. She put it down to his worldly travels and the foods he'd experienced in foreign ports. Today, afternoon tea would consist of fresh baked bread, home churned butter, and strawberry preserves. For dinner it would be lamb chops, green beans and potatoes. Nothing fancy in either case – just simple English fare. She'd prepare something more exotic for dinner tomorrow.

Mid morning the Captain came downstairs dressed in pressed slacks and a crisply ironed white shirt. She'd made tea, and was about to pour a cup, when she heard the clatter of hooves, as they slowed and stopped directly outside. Looking through the window she exclaimed, "I think that will be a carriage for you, Sir." A forceful knock on the front door had her hastily heading out into the hall and opening it.

A gentleman in a bedraggled foul weather coat holding an enormous black umbrella stood there and asked "'Morning, my lady. Is the Captain in, perchance?"

"Yes, Sir. Please step inside out of this horrible weather. I'll go fetch him for you."

The visitor was an envoy from Admiralty House bringing a request for the Captain's presence there. No doubt it was in order to learn about his next assignment, and he had actually been expecting the summons. He finished his tea, retrieved his jacket from upstairs, donned his heavy coat and hat, and strode briskly to the carriage, sheltering under the coachman's umbrella as he climbed inside.

He had no inkling of the surprise awaiting him.

Chapter 4

The rain was diminishing slightly and the clip clop of the horse's hooves on the cobblestones lulled the Captain into a relaxed state. The carriage chosen for his transportation was ornate inside, in recognition of his status. Red velvet cushions padded both the seat and backrest, gilt framing adding an almost royal touch. Fine-grained leather lined the inside of both doors, the handles being polished brass. Clear windows in the doors allowed him protected views of the rain-soaked street, numerous urchins and workers scurrying out of the way of the carriage in its determined progress. The coachman was clearly an experienced and cautious driver, for he kept up a steady but careful pace, one at which the horse was unlikely to experience any slippage.

The Captain noticed and appreciated professionalism wherever it occurred. It was a trait developed at his father's side, although it was his mother who encouraged him to always voice his praise to the source if appropriate. In her view of the world too many people criticized others' actions and too few voiced approval. She often quoted part of one of her favorite proverbs, "Praise makes good people better." The Captain remembered her oft-repeated story about her one visit to the House of the Admiralty Lords. It was when her husband had been promoted to the position of Admiral, the ceremony in his honor where he received his commendation and robes. She was so proud of him, and never ceased to relish her visit with the highest Sea Lords. It took little prompting to have her describe the finery of the room where the investiture was carried out, the required bowing and deference, and the delightful savories and champagne offered at the reception which followed.

And now the Captain was once again climbing the front steps of the yellow brick building, heading for the library to await a summons to the Admiral's suite. The building had been erected in 1788, designed as more of a residence than a suite of offices. It was the official residence of the First Lord of the Admiralty, and could also be used by Prime Ministers at times when 10 Downing St. was being renovated.

After a fifteen minute wait a uniformed aide appeared and led the Captain to the tall massive doors of the Admiral's study. He opened them, announced the Captain, and ushered him inside. Admiral Stephen Pennington rose from behind his desk and strode across the plush carpeted floor with hand extended in greeting. "Captain Fielding, thank you for coming on this miserable morning. Do take a seat, and I'll have tea brought in."

Once tea and small talk had been dispensed with, the Admiral stood and walked to the tall windows, his hands clasped behind his back, and his head pensively bowed,. "We wondered if you'd be interested in a different type of assignment this time, Captain. Please hear me out.

"For twenty years now we've been sending shiploads of convicts to Botany Bay in Australia. The current day media revel in lauding the removal of these terrible criminals who are plaguing our streets and upsetting our citizens with their outrageous deeds. The real issue, as you may well know, is that the growing crime sprees are the result of hungry citizens who cannot find jobs, and resort to stealing. Food in most cases, but often smaller items that can be pawned to buy food. Yes, there are prostitution and beatings and murders, but these are a mere fraction of the cases resulting in convictions. The justice system, flawed as it is, cannot handle more local incarcerations, as the gaols are essentially full. Thus, more and more convicts are being transported to the Antipodes. We, the Admiralty Lords, in co-operation with Government officials, are being forced to commandeer more and more merchantmen ships and convert them into transportation prisons.

"What is disturbing us greatly from examination of the records returned from Sydney is the high death rate of prisoners during the long voyages south. We have kept from public knowledge the shocking circumstances of the second fleet in which 30% of the 1000 prisoners died enroute or at landing, with another 10% dying from ship-precipitated conditions and diseases in the following eight months -- an embarrassing record to be kept hidden as long as possible.

"Even with more stringent rules of passage and care, we still have deaths of nearly 5% on any ship. That doesn't make the Navy feel very proud. It's bad enough that we are sending men and women, who in the main have committed essentially trivial crimes, so far away. But to treat them so poorly enroute is uncalled for.

"We're looking for a new set of captains who will regard the health and safety of their prisoners with nearly the same priority as they would treat their crews. There are prominent lawmakers in Europe already heavily criticizing us for how the convicts are transported. Unseemly deaths along the way add poignant fuel to their arguments.

"You have an outstanding reputation, Captain Fielding, as a sailor, taskmaster, and tactician. You show compassion, excellent judgment, and what we insiders acknowledge is superb common sense. We may appear high and mighty to the populace at large, and while we are men of authority, we understand the minutiae of managing massive ships under sail. We think you are the kind of Captain who can help restore our faith in the ability to command in far off waters.

"There is a barque scheduled to leave out of Gravesend in two weeks that is planned to have an unusual contingent of prisoners – 90 women and about 110 men. This will be one of the first vessels with such a mix of sexes aboard. So saying, it will need new dimensions of management and control both above and below deck.

"The Lords unanimously feel you are precisely the right man to captain this vessel. We hope you'll agree."

Captain Fielding had been listening patiently, deliberately holding back his questions and thoughts. He and the Admiral had developed a mutual respect over the years and he was certain that the Admiral had been the one who had proffered his name for consideration. As comfortable as he was with plying the north Atlantic to America, he was intrigued from a seaman's perspective with the potential challenge of crossing two major oceans in an extended voyage. The Admiral's added concern of minimizing convict deaths enroute was a totally new aspect, as the ships to and from America had been freighters with limited paying passengers on board.

"Sir, I sincerely appreciate the confidence the Lords have in me, and I am flattered by this request. I am most willing to undertake the role described, although I would like to see for myself the records you describe, and if possible talk to a few of the captains and surgeons who have sailed previously to Botany Bay."

"Your request has been anticipated, Captain, and I thank you for your concurrence in this assignment. I have every faith that you will be successful in helping change our record for the better. If you will return at 2 pm tomorrow afternoon, I will arrange to have two Captains who are in town to be available, along with two militia commanders. The following day I will have the surgeons present. If you know a surgeon with whom you would prefer to work, I would be happy to arrange his participation as well. Thank you again."

"Well Sir, there is a surgeon named Dr. Thomas Browning in whom I have a lot of confidence, although he has never been in charge of so many prisoners. I would like to talk to him to gauge his interest. As far as I know he is still stationed in Portsmouth, so having him come to London could possibly delay departure depending on his arrangements."

"If he turns out to be the man you want so be it. We have the authority to hold a boat for a few days if necessary. I will send an emissary at once to arrange his visit here. Once again I thank you for your commitment."

The Admiral walked over to the massive doors, opened them and held his hand out again. "Always a pleasure, Captain Fielding. Until tomorrow."

As he waited for the carriage to be brought around from the nearby stables, the Captain wondered what his mother would think were she still living. No doubt she'd be proud of the Lords' recognition of her son's capabilities, but probably aghast at the revelations about the second fleet voyage. And she'd probably have strong opinions about how women convicts should be treated. "I wonder what exactly she'd suggest," the Captain thought to himself. "Maybe Mrs. Hutchinson will have some practical ideas."

Chapter 5

Mrs. Hutchinson greeted the Captain at the front door, helping him off with his coat and hat, both of which had stayed relatively dry under the protection of the coachman's umbrella. His boots, however, were quite damp. She brought them inside to the sitting room and placed them in front of the small fire blazing in the grate. "Sit and warm up, Captain, while I go put the kettle on. I want to hear about your next ship."

Warmed on the outside by the fire and inside by tea, the Captain commenced his tale. "Something totally new and exciting ahead, Mrs. Hutchinson. They've asked me to captain one of the convict transports to Botany Bay. Many ships have already made the voyage but apparently too many prisoners are dying along the way. They want me to make changes to remedy the problem.

"But, they've added a significant challenge – I'm to manage a mixed load of 90 women and 110 men. I've seen how hundreds of male prisoners are housed in the hulks on the Thames, so I already have a few ideas of what might be appropriate to look after them. But I've never even been in the female section of any prison, so this will be a major learning experience. I'm to have my choice of surgeons and I'll be able to pick the leaders of my crew. My stipend will be enhanced, and on return there'll be a considerable extra reward if I deliver 99% of the prisoners in a healthy state. But there's so much to be done in short order, and I'm afraid it will mean you will be alone here much longer than in my past absences."

"Well, congratulations, Captain. Clearly the Admiralty Lords have a lot of confidence in you, and I have no doubt you will be successful. When is your planned departure? Will it be from Gravesend, and will you be picking up prisoners at other ports, like Plymouth or Cork? Oh my, I must check your clothes and uniforms closely to ensure they are in perfect condition. One thing I insist – you must buy that new dressing gown before you go, no waiting until you come back, as we had discussed. I will check with your tailor tomorrow to see what he might be able to offer. When do you leave again?"

"Unfortunately the ship is due to sail in two weeks, which gives us precious little time to organize, although I have been promised that the date can be moved back a few days if necessary. I am to return tomorrow afternoon to look at some of the records and talk to other captains who have travelled the route.

"Thank you for thinking about my clothes, including the robe. That's very kind of you. As I understand it, the trip could well take 140 days, and that's if weather conditions are good. I'd probably need up to 60 days in Sydney to effect any repairs and to arrange cargo to bring back, so that means I'll be gone over 11 months. Oh my, that's a long time to be gone and to leave you on your own, Mrs. Hutchinson. Would you prefer to stay in a boarding house instead where there'd be more people around?"

"You mean, rent out your house to complete strangers who could totally ruin it with lack of care?" Her voice took on a tone of utter disdain. "I won't have it, Captain!

"I will obviously miss you but I'm sure I can handle it. Don't spare another thought over it. I will be fine." She turned her head so the Captain wouldn't see the slight indication of misgiving and concern that momentarily crossed her face. Actually, she realized she would miss him immensely. She doted on looking after him. What really would she do for eleven months plus in his absence? The house would seem incredibly empty. "Ah well," she thought. "I'll simply have to work something out. Maybe a young girl boarder? I'll raise it again later."

"You know what worries me most, Mrs. Hutchinson? The women convicts. I have no experience with them, aside from watching a couple of ugly hangings in the past, and those don't help me in any way. Maybe Dr. Browning, the surgeon, will have good ideas."

Mrs. Hutchinson looked up from her tea abruptly. "I might have something to offer, Sir. Sometimes at the conclusion of formal catered events at the Academy, my sister would take left-over food to the local gaol, where she distributed it to both male and female inmates. She would cry in telling me about the wretched conditions the poor souls endured and would say, 'If only they had something to occupy the hours of each day, time would pass more quickly.' I asked her once what she was thinking about, and she rattled off a number of items. Let me see what I can remember...."

"One of the items was books. Stories they might read to one another, especially for the women, plus any that would be good for schooling the children incarcerated with them. Since nearly all of the female prisoners had at some point made their own clothes, they requested needles and thread, and pieces of cotton or woolen cloth that could be used to patch existing clothes, or if the material was in sufficient quantity, sew new ones. I don't remember specific wishes from the men, as Eliza and I empathized much more with the women. Can you find out tomorrow more information about the prisoners? Are they young girls or older women? Are they literate? Books won't help if they can't read.

"Forgetting items that might help with creature comforts, you may want to know more about the prisoners in any event. Are there any violent murderers or rapists among the men? What sort of professions do they come from – are there specific skills that might be useful on a long voyage, or are they all labourers? And among the women, what positions did they hold before conviction – maids, seamstresses, other occupations? And what sort of crimes did they commit – if most were 'ladies of the night,' you will have your hands more full than if they are mainly petty thieves. The more you know, the better prepared you will be for unseemly behavior below decks, Sir."

"Mrs. Hutchinson, you are wise beyond your years. Thank you for those suggestions…"

She interrupted him. "Board games, puzzles, hair-brushes… Whoops. Sorry, Sir, I just remembered other things the prisoners wanted. My apologies for interrupting."

"Great memory recall, Mrs. Hutchinson. Those are wonderful ideas. I will make a note of them. Now where is my writing tablet?"

"Bibles, Sir. Bibles. You will need Bibles. Not only for women. I'm sure that many of the prisoners, both sexes, will search for truth and redemption through the Lord. Maybe writing paper with pencils, and drawing paper and crayons.

"But even as I offer these ideas I wonder whether the government will agree to furnish them. After all aren't these people supposed to be the dregs of society, and be denied any of the privileges that ordinary citizens might receive? That's how most of today's newspapers seem to envisage the poor souls. I think you might want to double check, Captain, before requesting."

"You are a very astute woman, Mrs. Hutchinson. Except for the dangers of the voyage I'd take you along with me. You'd be an inspiration aboard. You've made me think that I need to make a trip to the attic. I had an extra trunk stored there. I'm sure it is still there but I wonder what condition it is in."

"Why would you want to look at an old trunk, Sir? You current trunk will hold all your clothes and papers adequately. It is stored in easy reach at the end of your bed, as you must know."

"Of course, of course, Mrs. H. But your warnings about the Government's attitude over niceties for convicts is most relevant. Perhaps I could take on board an extra trunk full of games, books, fabric and seamstress instruments that I will have personally bought and paid for. If supplying those things will make my life as captain easier, why shouldn't I bring them along? Want to go shopping with me the day after tomorrow?"

"You are such a generous man Captain. My soul sings with your heart-felt care for your fellow man and consideration of his plight. You will be a hero to the prisoners in many ways. And I would be proud to accompany you to the stores to help select appropriate entertainment and educational items for your charges."

Little did the Captain realize how much new learning he was about to receive.

Chapter 6

Mrs. Hutchinson cleared the plates from breakfast and rushed upstairs to put on her best dress. If she was to be out and about in the finest shops in London with the Captain, she wanted to be dressed like a woman of fashion. She was looking forward to directing the Captain to the relevant stores. She smiled at the memory of his statements last evening.

"I have no doubt Mrs. H. that there are many shops that could serve our needs, but you will know the ones where selection and service are paramount, so I'm delighted you are willing to guide me. I'll arrange for a carriage to be here at 10 am. We can shop until 1 pm, when I will carry on to Admiralty House and have the driver bring you home with our parcels."

It was clear that he was not sure which stores would stock the items he wanted, but she knew from looking in the shop windows and gossiping with other women exactly where they needed to go. The Captain instructed the coachman to follow any directions Mrs. Hutchinson might present and indicated he expected the man to help load and treat deferentially any parcels brought out through the doors of the stores. The recent creation of Regent Street, crossing Regent Circus North, was the first of many destinations, especially targeting the booksellers there. Purchases of ten children's textbooks in various subjects, fifteen children's story books, and twenty Bibles left two merchants very happy.

Next came the selection of fabrics. Here the Captain waited outside Layton & Shears while Mrs. Hutchinson made her selections. She explained to the Captain that she stayed far away from the expensive but gorgeous embossed satin and bombazeen, arguing that most of the female convicts would probably be of a lower class, and used to cotton and woolen garments. The only splurging was for a few yards of pretty English poplins. She also bought sewing needles, knitting needles, scissors, thread, and multiple skeins of worsted wool for darning along with several little wooden darning eggs.

It took several stores to complete the selection of board games and playing cards. Since the Captain himself played chess, he splurged on an expensive Calvert chess set, but otherwise they bought peg solitaire, the game of the goose, and several differently designed boards for checkers. At the end, the carriage was bulging with boxes and the Captain wondered if he might need an extra trunk to carry everything with him. When he raised the thought with Mrs. Hutchinson she dismissed it immediately saying she would pack the extra trunk at home and it would have plenty of space for the items they'd bought.

"One last thing Captain…" she exclaimed as the squeezed between parcels stacked on the seats. The thought lay unfinished as moving through the crowded interior space caused her leg and skirt to rub against the Captain's knee. She raised a hand to her mouth in pardon and interrupted herself "Excuse me, Sir, I do apologize. I did not mean to be familiar."

The Captain smiled a broad grin and responded with a happy lilt to his voice. "Dear Mrs. H. I take no offence. In fact your touch reminded me of pleasures of long ago. You've made me feel quite young again, so do not despair. Thank you."

Mrs. H. blushed, but as she started to turn away, the Captain reached for one of her hands and kissed it gently on the back. It was a gesture of heartfelt thanks and respect, and summed up his unspoken appreciation of everything she meant to him. She looked into his eyes and immediately realized that the intimacy she sometimes craved was hidden there, but in a different form than what she dreamed about. She relaxed in the understanding of the degree of care implicitly revealed in his action. A lovely warmth spread through her heart.

Composing herself, she touched the Captain's shoulder without hesitation. "That one last thing I started to mention Captain…. Your dressing gown. I've asked the coachman to take us to your tailor."

"You do look after me, Mrs. H. I thank you again. What a delightful excursion this has become."

The Captain enjoyed his housekeeper telling the tailor in no uncertain terms what fabric, color, and style would be used to make his new gown. The poor man behind the tables was initially taken aback, but his huffy demeanor changed once he realized that Mrs. Hutchinson had very good taste, knew her materials, and was *au fait* with the latest fashions. As he led the Captain to a side room in order to take measurements, Mrs. Hutchinson found herself thinking about her long lost son. She had taken him to a tailor once, to buy the fabric for his first dressing gown, which she had then sewed from scratch back home. She remembered

Edward's anger and passive defiance in the store reflecting how much he hated the experience. Years afterwards, he told her that he felt she had talked about him over his head to the tailor, almost as if he weren't there, and that he felt the tailor was snooty, unfriendly, and condescending. She sighed with the recollection, wondering what the Captain might have been like as a little boy taken on his first visit to a tailor. Probably much more accepting and gracious than her son.

Her mind was still searching the memories of yesteryear when the tailor and the Captain emerged. "Penny for your thoughts, Mrs. H." the Captain offered. "You seemed a long way away."

"Aye, that I was, Sir. Thinking about my boy and the robe I made for him so long ago. I wonder where he might be these days and whether he has fine clothes like you, Sir. Please forgive me."

"I understand Mrs. H. I really do. Come, our shopping day is done. You must head home and I will enjoy a brisk walk to Admiralty House. You have done me a wonderful service and I am in your debt. I'm sure I will have interesting news to share when I return this evening."

Indeed, that was definitely to be the case, but there would also be news that would not be shared.

Chapter 7

There were many topics the Captain wanted to discuss with the other two boat Captains, and he had made out a list so he wouldn't forget any. As expected, they were anxious to recount their experiences, but the Captain quickly came to the conclusion that they were minimizing the trials and problems of their voyages. The safe topics were the ships themselves, the seas, the winds, the temperature, the errors of latitude and longitude measurement, the accuracy of the charts, and the descriptions of ports used in both South America and Africa. It was when they started talking about the quantity and quality of food, rations, sailor competence and insubordination, disease, relationships with the militia onboard, and convict discipline, that the Captain detected unease and wariness in both of the Captains and a clear reluctance to provide full details.

He was aware that they did not want to openly criticize their headquarter-based superiors, but the undertone of their remarks made it clear that they felt their concerns had not been well understood, and certainly not heeded. They seemed uncomfortable addressing the issues of the routes approved by the Admiralty, the provisions, and the conditions for the prisoners. The Captain was heartened by their empathy for the convicts, but disturbed by the lack of detail around other misgivings. He kept his thoughts to himself so as not to embarrass the men, but anticipated he would pursue the topics with extra vigor when talking to the surgeons the following day.

His conversations with the militia officers were relatively short and were confined to management of the prisoners. It was clear these men felt that by being placed in charge of prisoners they had been relegated to the least favorable military tasks. Their displeasure with higher command was clearly taken out on the prisoners, as they exhibited little flexibility in attitude or interest over the prisoners' plight. They enforced the rules with too much enthusiasm in the Captain's eyes, always using the upper limits for the number of whippings or days of confinement. Clearly these were 'individuals of small mind' wielding their limited amount of power with great self-satisfaction. The Captain dismissed them quickly, indicating his disgust by assuring them that they would have no place on his ship.

The shortness of the latter interviews gave him time to seek out the Admiral, who became available for consultation after less than a thirty minute wait. He now entered into earnest conversation about the prisoners he was to transport. The Admiral pulled a large leather binder from one of the drawers in his desk and referred to a plethora of loose sheets of paper as he attempted to answer the Captain's probing questions.

Of the 90 women to be traveling, two thirds had no prior convictions, and 30% had one conviction. Both men were surprised at the number with one or more convictions, having expected significantly fewer. It turned out that many of these were young mothers convicted of theft, but who had sometimes been let go after a short incarceration in order to look after multiple children, but then caught again.

In fact 81 of the women had been charged with theft, 7 were in for repeated run-ins for prostitution, 2 for vagrancy. The Captain sighed in relief to learn that no truly violent female criminals would be aboard. Another surprise came in learning that 70% of all the women were between the age of 17 and

34, and that many would have children with them. Because these women were clearly still of child-bearing age he wondered whether there was a hidden agenda to send them away for breeding purposes, since the Botany Bay population was over 95% male.

A pleasant finding was that more than 75% of the women were literate, and that their expertise covered 6 different trades, ranging from cook, to bookkeeper, to maid, and even governess. It was clear that the profiles of the women prisoners were a total mismatch to the stereotypes painted in the press of morally degenerate prostitutes and other lowly persons who were unskilled and illiterate.

The surprises continued in reviewing the qualities and backgrounds of the 110 male prisoners. A fifth of them were teenagers, and since 75% were under 30, the bulk, 60 men, ranged in age between 20 and 29. Three quarters were unmarried, nearly 50% could both read and write, with another 20% who could only read. Once again, the legend portrayed in the press of mentally-deficient individuals was clearly bogus. Nearly 30% indicated that they were labourers or farm labourers, although amongst the remaining 77 individuals, clerks and teachers dominated professional ranks while the remainder held trade skills of shoemakers, tailors, weavers, metalworkers, miners, and butchers. Although these latter male prisoners didn't know it at the time, they would be in demand on arrival in Sydney and relatively fortunate. The labourers would most likely go to chain gangs.

Pleased with his findings and anxious to get home after the long day, the Captain politely declined the Admiral's invitation for a glass of sherry, and headed outside to hail a coach. A light sprinkle had recently started falling, and carriages up and down the street were busy responding to the sudden rush of requests for transport. The Captain's driver made a smart U-turn and slowly headed back through the shopping district.

The pace was slow as coaches maneuvered to the edges of the roadways to pick up new passengers and then rejoined the traffic stream. Suddenly the Captain's carriage was tipped backwards as the horse reared up on his hind legs thoroughly frightened by a young man who rushed out of a shop door and collided with the animal. As the carriage righted itself, a shop steward came out the door and yelled "Thief, stop!" in a loud voice. The young man who had run into the horse and fallen had a large parcel under his arm, and now got to his feet and sprinted off down the street between the chaotic line of coaches.

Without hesitation the Captain opened his door, stepped out, and ran after the thief. He was really no match in speed for the young chap, who had a ten yard start. But the muddling carriage line created obstacles as carriages moved left and right to pick up patrons or head into the traffic stream with their passengers onboard. Several times the Captain lost sight of his charge as he dodged in and out between the transports. By anticipating the movements of carriages well ahead the Captain found himself gaining ground. Attempting to round a corner at speed the thief slipped and stumbled, his package rolling away. Once again he got to his feet, but the Captain was only a yard behind, and with an energetic burst of speed, launched himself through the air in what bystanders later called a rugby tackle and caught the man around his upper legs.

With his massive size and weight the Captain subdued the chap easily and was soon assisted by other men once he pronounced the man a thief.   The steward from the shop turned up and retrieved the parcel as a large crowd gathered in the light rain waiting for a constable to arrive. A youthful female onlooker turned to her companion and said quite loudly, "Cor, that gentleman ain't half strong. Look how big he is. Arms and legs like tree-trunks. Ooh, I wouldn't mind 'im sittin' on me... "   A couple of women tittered as the young lass' boyfriend grabbed her arm and hurriedly moved her on.

The shop clerk thanked the Captain over and over, and walked beside him to his carriage now waiting at the edge of the crowd.   He offered to have the Captain's coat and pants cleaned, as they were both quite a mess - very damp and dirty, with a small rip in one knee of the trousers. The Captain accepted the offer as the clerk shook hands with him, then urged his driver to head homeward as fast as the roads would allow.

His day had been full of good deeds and he had garnered a lot of valuable information at the Academy.

Things would look quite differently on the morrow, however, after discussions with the surgeons.

Chapter 8

"Your biggest problem, Captain, will be controlling the women prisoners." Sitting back, the Surgeon patted down the tobacco in his pipe and looked squarely into the Captain's eyes.

"And it doesn't matter how well you think you are doing, I warrant you will still have issues. The last ship I was on had only female prisoners. No male convicts, although there were 4 young male passengers in the paid cabins, and of course the guardsmen and sailors were men. That was enough.

"Now, I'm not talking specifically about sexual urges, although they are definitely part of the tension on board, but something you probably wouldn't think about back here in London. In our voyage the issue became more prevalent in the second half of the journey. Before departure most of the women had heard stories as to how they would be packed off on arrival in Sydney to the women's factory 15 miles away in Parramatta to sew clothes for convicts, and that they could be incarcerated there for years. Some of the smarter women realized that they would have a better life in Sydney if they arrived married.

"It started when we stopped in Cape Town to replenish supplies and carry out minor repairs. The ship was anchored and stable, the weather was fine, and the women were allowed on deck for longer periods than before in order to exercise, and to have a break from their cramped quarters. Simultaneously the sailors were more relaxed. Some took shore leave, others stayed on the boat. The paying passengers went ashore and stayed in a local hotel. The militia's focus was to make sure no convict jumped overboard and tried to swim to escape. Surprisingly, one woman did so and nearly made it, save for the fact that the first person she ran into onshore was a policeman.

"A number of the more precocious women actively pursued the sailors and one of the guards, who was quite a handsome fellow. The head cook also received attention when he wasn't ashore buying supplies. We had a little over 200 women on board, plus children, and according to my observations five relationships took on serious overtones over the following six weeks. There were numerous sexual dalliances of course, but in fact before we reached a point south of Cape Leeuwin on the southwest tip of Australia, three couples asked the Captain to perform marriages upon them."

Captain Fielding pondered this information for a minute and then stated, "That doesn't sound like a major problem to me, Doctor. Three newly married women on arrival, and a bunch of others sexually satisfied. What am I missing?"

"Ah Captain Fielding, I'm sorry I didn't make myself clear. When you set sail you will have 110 men besides crew and guards. Remember I only had 4, and as paying passengers they were strictly off-limits for the prisoners. In your case I suspect you will have many more couples coming to you, simply because more men are available. Plus the male convicts are also aware that arriving in a married state will make them appear more stable to the authorities and better able to create a reasonable living in the new country."

"Thank you, that does make sense. I do understand what you are saying now. So let's talk about prisoner quarters, general conditions, diet and health, instead. First, diseases. Are women more prone to certain illnesses than men, putting aside of course that there may be some from pregnancy complications?"

"Surprisingly Captain, when we compare numbers, disease resulting in death onboard occurs more frequently in men than women. We think that's due to the fact that the male convict ships are usually overcrowded and men pay less attention to their diet. The female prisoner ship my colleague was on had only 200 women. I was on its next trip and we had nearly 300 men. It's clear to us that less crowding would be one thing that would alleviate disease and subsequent death during the trip. The worst disease is of course scurvy. 120 days at sea without enough citrus offerings can be devastating. Our own Navy ensures enough lime juice onboard our ships for nearly 6 months at sea.

"As you probably know, in order to cut down total voyage length to Sydney, the Admiralty is seeking to avoid the stops in Rio or Cape Town, where extra citrus fruits can be bought. I don't mind telling you, that on my next trip I will do everything I can to convince the Captain to put in to Cape Town.

"We are required to keep detailed logs of patients we treat. Some doctors record diarrhea, dysentery and erysipelas as causes of death. To me however, these are all symptoms of scurvy, and I use that a lot more than others in my 'cause of death' column. Typhoid, constipation ulcers, scrofula, and diseases of the respiratory and musculoskeletal systems round out the other causes of deaths that apply to both sexes.

"Among women we often see depression, especially after giving birth, and not just with stillbirths. They also exhibit emotional and psychological problems, or hysteria, far more than men. Basically from leaving families behind. The best treatment is usually offered by the women around them providing comfort and support.

"Men become surly, women become sad. The only joy occurs when a mother gives live birth, and I'm sorry to say, often the joy doesn't last. The mother's strength and diet, her ability to produce milk, adequate clothing, and clean conditions are essential for babies to survive. Your saddest duty Captain will be burying a child at sea...

"Well gentlemen, no one could criticize you for skirting bad news.... What other problems should I be aware of?"

"Sir, sanitation is an issue. Make sure the latrines are emptied regularly, bedding must be taken topside and aired every week, clothes should be washed frequently, and the decks below kept clean. Have your surgeon check frequently for scabies and lice. Good ventilation is imperative but people get lazy about managing it. If you can secure a few extra cats before departure that will help with the rat problem, but you will still have cockroaches. Catching them in pools of molasses uses up that sweet ingredient but works well. Collect rainwater whenever the heavens open. The original water placed on board here in London will go bad once you pass through the tropics and are in the Southern Atlantic. And make sure the pens for the animals and fowls are built strongly enough to counter major gales."

"Well, gentlemen, you have provided quite an education for me. I really appreciate your considered opinions and suggestions. They seem most logical and appropriate. I shall make notes at home this evening, for I am sure I would forget your advice should I not record it expeditiously. Do either of you know Dr. Browning, who resides in Portsmouth at the moment?"

One of the men spoke up saying, "Oh yes, Sir, Dr. Browning and I were at Edinburgh University, getting our Doctorates of Medicine in the same year. He's a very competent physician. I didn't know that he had an interest in serving in the Navy. Is he your choice for Surgeon on your ship? If he comes to London I would certainly enjoy the chance to meet with him again. Perhaps you'd be so kind as to present him with this extra calling card of mine?"

"I would be happy to do so, Doctor. Thank you both for your time and input. I am truly indebted, but feel much better prepared to take on the daunting task you have laid before me." So saying he proffered his hand to one then the other, and ushered them out of the suite.

The men smiled knowingly to one another as they walked down the front steps of the building to their carriage, confident that no Captain taking on a load of convicts of both sexes had any idea of what really lay ahead.

They understood how natural primitive human urges would overwhelmingly govern onboard behavior, especially after a couple of months at sea.

Chapter 9

"As you can see Mrs. Hutchinson, I have my work cut out for me. And I suspect that there is much still that I have not been told, but will learn first-hand along the way. Probably the Botany Bay Captains and Surgeons welcome another into their ranks, but no doubt feel that I have to go through the 'rites of passage' on my own, as they did, to prove my worthiness. Snobbery clearly still exists in our upper classes.

"But there, I think I've told you everything I learned these past two days. This is going to be a trial Mrs. H., I warrant. But then again, it would probably be very boring if there weren't some unknown challenges ahead.

"Thank you for that excellent roast lamb dinner. Clearly one more thing I will miss for far too long on this voyage. Please join me in another glass of this excellent red from Italy. I must make sure the cook has several cases of this particular wine on board, if only just for me. The tales I've shared with you make me feel that there will be instances on the voyage when I will definitely need to console and re-fortify myself. And this fine elixir may be my best companion in such instances."

Mrs. Hutchinson quickly rose and noisily gathered up plates from the table, turning away so the Captain would not see the moisture forming in the lower rims of her grey-blue eyes. She was hesitant to respond to the Captain's musings, implicitly realizing that if she did, her voice would be sure to quaver and reveal her sudden discomfort. She was surprised at how her feelings for the man had unexpectedly touched her soul with the re-awakened comprehension that he would be gone so long. They'd talked about arrangements for his absence but for unknown reasons his pending departure had suddenly become more imminent.   Clearly she was anticipating heartfelt misery at his being gone.

She bustled out of the kitchen and took refuge in the parlor. There, however, control left her and she sat in one of the high-backed stuffed chairs, drew a handkerchief from her bosom, hung her head, and let the tears flow freely. Her sobs resounded in the hallway. The Captain followed her a moment later, his brows creased with concern and empathy. He stood quietly beside her for a few seconds, then bent down and put his arm around her shoulders, holding her gently against his side.

"Thank you for your tender heart and concern for my welfare, Mrs. H. You are an incredible person and wonderful woman. I am blessed with your unselfish support and loyalty. I'm sorry that I probably haven't fully appreciated your tenderness. You are a very special person in my life, filling a void that other family men never know.   You espouse gracefulness, devotion, and true femininity. Sometimes I ask myself why I've not approached you for a more personal union."

Anne's crying had stopped and her heart was fluttering as she absorbed the Captain's words. A welcome warmth started to spread throughout her body. She slowly twisted her head towards the Captain, leaning into his hug, relishing the strength of his hold.   And became subtly aware of a change in his physique as she unthinkingly brushed her hand across his loins. Unspoken words were silently mouthed by both, and Anne stood and they embraced fervently, the Captain's huge arms squeezing her to his frame. She stretched up and breathed softly against his cheek, conscious of her breasts appreciating the crush against his firm "gentleman boxer's" torso. As his physical interest became more pronounced she whispered: "You make me feel like a young woman with certain needs again, Captain. I think you might be interested to show me your quarters."

Several hours later, Mrs. H. tiptoed out of the Captain's room and headed downstairs. She closed the kitchen door and hummed a sweet refrain as she cleared and washed the dinner plates and pots and pans. A broad smile reflected her happiness, her disposition more cheery than it had been for days. Clearly, she remonstrated with herself, she had unwittingly been dreading the Captain's departure far more than she had been willing to admit. She would still miss him, she realized, but the intimacy they had shared would hold for as long as she needed it to. Based on the newness and love just experienced, even a year could pass by without anxiety.

A message from Admiralty House the following day indicated that Dr. Browning would be arriving in London that afternoon and would welcome the chance to meet with the Captain the next morning. While Mrs. H. sorted out the Captain's clothes, washing those with even the slightest amount of soil and pressing everything to the highest Navy standards, the Captain cleaned his pistol and thoroughly checked his Hadley's Quadrant, which was used to compute longitude at sea. He retrieved his precious dirk and the epaulettes for his coat out of the bottom drawer of the dresser. Mrs. H.

refreshed the epaulettes and sewed them in place on his jacket, but he himself took his knife to the grinder to be sharpened and polished.

Unbeknownst to the Captain, Dr. Browning's wife had passed away six months prior and as a consequence he readily accepted joining the Captain on his new voyage. He looked forward to filling his days with new challenges and moving out of the sorrow and grief that accompanied him every day. His only request was that the Captain call for him in Portsmouth so he could optimize his time there selling his house and furnishings and settling his affairs before departure to the Antipodes. As much as he had dearly loved his wife and cherished the memories of her, he felt that the coming days at sea would put his life with her gently behind him, and allow him to pursue a new life experience, albeit ill-defined, and definitely not without risk.

A new life was definitely to govern his future, but in no way that he could have predicted.

Chapter 10

The 'Surrey' rocked uneasily against the dock at Gravesend as the Thames reversed current. The lines to the bollards alternately slackened and tautened, and constant groans and creaks arose from the hull scraping against the dock walls. Completed earlier in the year at Whitby on the River Esk, she had passed her sea-worthiness tests in the North Sea with flying colors. A three-masted barque a little over 150 feet long with a 30 foot beam, she drew 16 feet when loaded, and presented an elegant picture against the backdrop of the town., Pungent smells of forest, coal, and pitch emanated from the deck and the hull planks. The latest practice of protecting the under-water part of the hull by wrapping it in copper sheathing had been applied, and the ship was the pride of its new owners. They'd been handsomely rewarded with the Navy's purchase of the 522 ton boat for transportation purposes. In order to make future boats even more acceptable to Naval command, they now stood dockside, watching the numerous modifications being made. A combination hospital/gaol had been added topside, and latrines fitted below, since humans as well as cargo were to be confined there. A new thin wooden wall would separate men and women prisoners. Pens and sheds for animals were being erected on deck, and more cannon were being added, according to the Navy's newest specifications.

It was late on a warm July day and the wharf men were sweating freely. While the windmills on top of Windmill Hill were spinning, no breeze penetrated the docks, due to the hill's overshadow of the dock area. The marshes to the east and west of the town were slowly drying, and every now and then when a gust of wind changed direction, their decaying smell rolled in. The noise was a discordant cacophony of sounds involving carpentry work on the boat, the stacking of crates on the wharf, shouts of the porters, the neighing of horses, and the barking of dogs. Despite the 27 mile distance from London, Captain Fielding had decided to visit and get his first glimpse of his ship. The owners had toured the decks with him, pointing out the significant components of construction, and had assured him that the canvas sails were all in perfect condition and fully ready to take on high winds...

For the past week the holds in the bottom of the ship had been filled with a variety of cargo destined for the new land. Industrial construction tools, agricultural implements, household tools, nails, screws, bags of corn and wheat seed, tents, firearms, bullets, fancy shingles and doors, hinges, pulleys, rope, and buckets.

In the afternoon, bunks and mattresses for the prisoners and sailors started to arrive. Tens of carts, each piled high, congregated on the wharf. Whereas there had been order at the entrance gates, on the wharf itself the scene was one of chaos. Horses bumped into each other, goods spilled, cart wheels locked onto other cart wheels, and drivers resorted to fisticuffs to settle trivial disputes on position and queue priority. Beneath his breath the Captain vowed that his ship would run far more efficiently than did business at the quayside.

A carpenter's apprentice crossed his path, headed for the ship, with long timbers precariously balanced on one shoulder, wobbling up and down and a little sideways. People stepped out of the way to avoid being hit by the wood. The Captain moved quickly and lifted the trailing ends of the lumber to stabilize them and marched behind the youngster up the boarding gangway. The chap had no idea he had been helped until he went to lower his bundle to the deck and found it supported from behind.

"'Cor, blimey, Sir, sorry! I didn't know you was there."

"You need to be more careful, lad, or next time you may arrive with no lumber, and find angry workers coming after you. You just missed hitting several people with your load."

The Captain shook his head and watched the master carpenter drag the apprentice off by the ear, giving him a harsh verbal lesson along the way. "Maybe it would be better if I didn't see the shenanigans going on here," the Captain thought to himself. But he stayed on anyway, observing that order slowly emanated out of chaos as goods were moved from the dock to the ship, and the piles on the wharf got smaller and smaller.

He'd spent several days at Admiralty House choosing the men who would be beneath him helping command the ship. The Sailing Master was in charge of navigation and the physical sailing of the ship. He directed the course and looked after the maps and instruments necessary for navigation. Since charts were primitive and often non-existent, his job was difficult, but absolutely vital. Captain Fielding applied more effort on this choice of officer than any other.

The Boatswain's function was to supervise the maintenance of the vessel and its supply stores. He was responsible for inspecting the sails and rigging each morning, and was also in charge of all deck activities, including weighing and dropping anchor and the handling of the sails. But it was the Quartermaster who actually managed the crew. He was often elected by the seamen, but in this case Captain Fielding selected his man and gave him authority to choose the Mates and 45 able-bodied seamen who would serve under him and actually ensure the running of the ship on a daily basis.

It was amazing how many details had to be organized and how little time was available. The Captain's biggest concern was that Dr. Browning would not be joining the boat until it docked at Portsmouth. While Portsmouth was only eighty miles southwest of London by road, it could take a week to sail there from Gravesend, depending on the weather.

In the southern environs of the North Sea, and in the English Channel, turbulent seas often prevailed, the journey along the coast being made more challenging if a nasty storm blew in. In any event this was a portion of the journey when many of the passengers were undoubtedly bound to be seasick, so it was imperative to have a Surgeon on board. Few Surgeons were interested in only taking on a short trip and after several interviews the Captain reluctantly accepted the application of a semi-retired 60 year old gentleman who was happy to get a free ride to visit relatives in Devon. Dr. Jamieson would just have to do.

Mrs. Hutchinson was in a dither, for she had misplaced one of the Captain's handkerchiefs, and it was to be the last item packed into his dress trunk. She traipsed upstairs for a third time, searching the Captain's rooms, but to no avail. Tears formed in her eyes, disbelief in her heart. She knew she hadn't packed it already. Maybe a cup of tea would help. Tomorrow he would leave for the long journey ahead, and despite all her inner fortitude she realized how much she would miss him. Handling his clothes and personal items had been much harder than previous times, due to how long he would be gone. Little would the Captain know, but there were a few tears in his trunk as well.

It was late afternoon before the handkerchief came to light. It had fallen off the edge of her own bed onto the Persian rug, and she couldn't recollect why it had ever even been in her room. Another conundrum she put down to the distress she felt at his departure. A large mystery box had been delivered shortly after lunch. Most unusually, the name of the shop was not shown and she figured the Captain had found some last minute item he needed on board. Parcels had been arriving throughout the week, most from Admiralty House. One had held a new speaking trumpet as a thank-you gift from the Admiral and his staff. The Captain had really appreciated it, as his old bullhorn had several dents in it and was showing its age. The new brass one would add to the sense of authority he would need on deck. Mrs. Hutchinson happily replaced the one she had already packed.

She prepared his favorite dinner for their last evening meal together. It was roast leg of lamb with mint sauce and dumplings, and she was in a surprisingly happy mood as they sat down to enjoy it. A fine red wine, light in color, complemented the meal and the couple sat chatting away as if they didn't have a care in the world. As the last of the bottle's contents disappeared, the Captain rose from the table and retrieved the package that had arrived earlier.

"Dear Mrs. H. I think my absence will create a void that will only become harder on you as the time I am gone lengthens. If by chance we meet a ship bound for London along the way I will send a note, but I can make no promises. I do have something for you in this box, however, that I hope will serve as a reminder of my indebtedness and feelings for you. Please go ahead and open it."

Her hands shaking, Anne grabbed scissors to cut the string holding the top down and reached inside. It took two hands to retrieve the item, which was wrapped in velvet. She placed it gently on the table and carefully unfolded the material. A joyous gasp registered both surprise and delight, and she turned to the Captain with a look of disbelief. "It is gorgeous," she whispered. "Incredibly beautiful. Where on earth did you find it? I've never seen anything like it. What exactly is it called?"

"Where I got it shall remain my secret, my dear. The only thing I will do is repeat what the mistress of the shop haughtily told me. Since she was so proud of her description I had her write it down for I would never be able to remember it perfectly. Here let me read to you." He reached inside his vest pocket and pulled out a perfumed card.

"It's called a heptagonal bag. That means seven joined pouches. The material that makes up the outside of each pouch is old rose moiré silk, and the rosette in the center of the steel cockade frame is also made of cut steel. The closure is steel and the inside lining of the pouches is white silk. As much as I would have liked to leave you with something made in England, this is from a French artist. It may be too delicate to actually use out on the streets, but I hope you will enjoy it anyway."

"Oh, Captain, it is truly unbelievable. I don't care if it is French. What beautiful artistry. And no, it will never see the outside world. It will sit on my dresser, open until you come home. It will be a constant reminder of you and your love. I thank you from the bottom of my heart. You are a gentleman of the highest standing."

With that she walked around the table and hugged the Captain with genuine tenderness and affection. He smiled at the kiss she planted on his forehead.

The following morning dawned windy and wet. The large cab arrived promptly at ten am and the driver put the three trunks inside rather than have them get soaked strapped to the back racks. There was still room for the Captain albeit a little cramped. Mrs. Hutchinson held her umbrella high as the Captain circled her waist with his free arm and drew her to him. "I shall think of you often, my dear. Do take care and let's hope the time passes quickly."

She reached up and stroked his cheek with her free hand. She knew her tears would come after the carriage turned the corner. For now she was smilingly brave. "God speed, my Captain. I shall await your return. Bon voyage and au revoir."

As the driver started to close the door she blew a kiss and couldn't resist one final thought.

"Please be careful and avoid the savages down there, dear Captain. With my sister and son well gone, you are all I have and live for in this world."

Part Two – the High Seas

Chapter 11

Captain Fielding and Dr. Jamieson stood at the deck rail watching the ungainly procession of prisoners slowly follow two red-coated militiamen through the dock area gates, around the main administrative building, and across the wharf to the foot of the gangway. The Captain descended the narrow planks, and the two guards gave half-hearted salutes in recognition.

"Beg pardon, Sir, 90 female prisoners for Botany Bay, Sir. Some with children. Permission to bring them aboard?"

"Granted. Take them below and remove the chains. Boatswain will show you their quarters."

The women staggered up the ramp to the deck, many casting hateful eyes at the Captain and members of the crew who had gathered to watch.   Children were dragged along, sometimes pushed by the woman next in line. Many of the adults had no shoes, their clothes were tattered and ill fitting, and their hair matted and coarse. The Surgeon watched them closely looking for obvious medical issues. Two heavily pregnant women caught his attention, and he ordered the guards to bring them to him once they were unchained. One wild-eyed woman spat at him, marking his trousers, and he noted her flaming red hair in his memory for later interrogation.   Most of the women presented dull, empty visages, reflecting the desperation they felt from their term in gaol and now close to departure to an unknown and unwanted future. Near the end of the line the monotony was broken by a young girl, probably not eighteen, who looked the Surgeon directly in his eyes and muttered beneath her breath, "We'll see what you are made of later, mister."

The guards handed over the lists of names with ages, birthplace, occupation, crimes, religion, and indications of ability to read or write, and while one guard stood above the under-deck hatchway the other three showed the women to their quarters. The two pregnant women were brought before the Surgeon who asked them how far along they were, whether they'd had children before, and what sort of issues they were experiencing. He checked their names on the list and wrote comments beside each one.

The male prisoners were not expected to appear until the following morning, so the Captain ordered the cook to prepare a good lunch for the women and suggested the Surgeon start checking them over to examine as many as possible before they sailed the following evening when the ride would probably get much rougher. He retreated to his cabin and undid the clasp on his 'extra' trunk, moving items aside to view the bolts of cloth neatly laid out by Mrs. Hutchinson at the base. Silent thanks ran through his mind.

The Surgeon glanced down the list of names in alphabetical order, put his slate aside and asked the guard to bring the spitting redhead to him. Sullen and defiant, her eyes flashing left and right, Molly Bridges realized by being singled out first, that she was in deep trouble. Little did she know just how vengeful the doctor could be. "Well, well Molly. Twenty one years old, from Liverpool. Protestant, can read but not write. In for repeated attacks and robberies of older men. You're a real charmer, Molly. Continuing your pastime on me as you came aboard."

Leaning forward, he slapped her hard enough that she fell to the floor whimpering. "Get up, you wretch. That's the start of your treatment. There'll be no lunch for you today and you'll spend the first 24 hours in the solitary cell without even bread and water. And for extra humiliation you'll be naked. Guard!"

As the guard opened the door Molly tried to run out but the guard tripped her and she went down again, clearly in pain as she fell backwards, striking the wooden ridge frame beneath the door. "Take her to the solitary cell, no food or water, disrobe her and bring her belongings back here. I'll examine her again in 24 hours. And bring me Eleanor Andrews, first name on the list."

One by one he checked the women for fever, respiratory infections, bruises, cuts, scars and fractures from beatings or other mistreatment, missing teeth and other oral conditions, skin lesions, and various internal problems such as constipation, diarrhea, menstrual issues, and sexually related conditions. Children brought along were also examined, and all conditions and treatment programs were written in the logs.

By mid-afternoon he'd examined 15 more of the women, handing out medication to 7 adults and 2 children. He was pleasantly surprised at their general health, and so reported to the Captain. There was one older woman with what was possibly pneumonia, and another with gonorrhea, and two children with fever – source unknown.   Other everyday internal discomfort symptoms were normal in incidence but none were serious.

After a break the doctor went back to his quarters and saw three more prisoners. The fourth to arrive, Margaret Ebbit, caused him a wry smile as she stepped across the threshold and recognition followed.   "Ah, Miss mutterer. Would you care to repeat your welcome-aboard comments?"   On a closer look, he had to give her credit.   She'd obviously had someone braid her hair into a single pigtail, so that her young face, which was essentially unblemished, seemed to have a freshness about it that was totally absent in the others. As well, the lass was smiling in a coquettish way that was not unattractive. She had apparently survived gaol incarceration better than many of the others.

 As the doctor dipped his head to read about her background, she quietly stepped out of her clothes, jumped up on the examining table and moved her legs wide apart. "You need to check me thoroughly doctor. I'm looking forward to it. Please start with my better parts."

As a practicing physician the doctor had seen it all before, but was still surprised at this girl's audacity. Not a prostitute according to the prisoner listing, rather a minister's daughter who'd stolen small icons from various churches (other than her father's) and pawned them for cash to buy food for poor parishioners. A puzzling mixture of good and bad intentions. When she was finally apprehended, it had required a female policewoman to retrieve the stolen goods from a body cavity, one which was now fully on display. The doctor asked his set of usual questions, finding the girl to be in better shape than any of her peers he'd checked earlier.

As he stopped writing on his clipboard Margaret got down, knelt in front of the doctor and hastily undid the buttons on his pants. His interest was obvious and she made short work of satisfying him.   As she dressed herself, she murmured softly, "I guess we did find out what you are made of after all doctor. Weakness, like all men."

The good doctor saw one more convict, then sought out the Captain, suggesting a stroll to one of the pubs in town for refreshments. They walked along the waterfront together, watching the Thames roll out to the North Sea at the start of its ebb stage.

"We'll go with the ebb about an hour later than this tomorrow, doctor. Let's hope the elements will be kind to us as we head out and allow the crew to become familiar with the ship at a non-urgent pace. I trust my officers but know nothing about the capabilities of the seamen they have selected. I will say that at least so far I haven't seen any of them drunk or asleep at their stations. I may hold back their rum rations until we dock in Portsmouth to keep them alert. They won't like me, but it wouldn't be the first time."

"I don't think you need the crew to 'like' you, Captain. If they 'respect' you that's the best you can aim for. There's bound to be tough situations along the way where they will simply have to follow orders, whether they agree with them or not. You are the supreme authority on board and your word is undeniable. At most you need to be fair when disputes or disciplinary situations arise. But you know that, I'm sure."

"Let me ask you something, doctor. The Navy has its rules and they only change with substantial evidence of need. One of the rules I am not convinced about is the absolute segregation of male and female prisoners. In the world at large, men and women exist together, travel together, often live together. Why do the authorities think that the prisoner class is so different that its members should always be separated?   I wonder whether such separation fosters discontent,   since   it's   the   opposite   of   natural   living conditions."

"I must admit, Captain, that I've never been on a ship with mixed sexes. And I've only been on one ship that had entirely female prisoners.   But I do understand your question. It's an astute observation, and of course may be worth a little test on the trip ahead once you leave English shores. All I can say is that there are natural proclivities for men and women to be together. Social companionships take different forms. Men and men, especially in business and sports, women and women in factories and teaching for example, and of course men and women in friendship and marriage. Children are only brought into this world through male and female union, and both sexes seek such, but also seek pleasure. In fact I had ample evidence of that this afternoon. One young lady enjoyed flaunting her sexual interests. I have no doubt she won't be the only one."

"A related thought I have is that any pair that has a strong desire to be together for coupling purposes, will probably find a way in any event. If such union keeps them happy, and eases tensions, why not remove obstacles, as long as others are not hurt. I will check on how Dr. Browning feels as well once he joins the ship in Portsmouth. I do have some other new ideas that I will test once we are on the high seas and the boredom of routine is affecting everyone."

"Probably best not to tell me about those other ideas, Captain, in case I ever get asked awkward questions by Admiralty officials. And I seem to have already forgotten what we were talking about before. Tomorrow morning the male convicts will be placed in their area below decks. Tell me are you going to address the men separately from the women or all together?"

"Together in one large group when the men arrive, and before they go below. I want every prisoner to hear the same rules. I'll make sure I tell the militia commander in advance."

The last of the animals and supplies were loaded the next morning, and an eerie silence fell across the dock on completion. The empty carts had disbursed and the wharf hands who remained lounged against the storage sheds or on broken packing cases and bales littering the area. Dark clouds blew overhead in front of the wind, which had switched direction from the previous day and was strong enough to blow smaller pieces of torn sacks, bits of coal, and strands of straw high above the masts and out to sea. The scene had an ominous feel about it as the wind swirled across the ship's deck in dust-filled gusts. Superstitious sailors among the crew became apprehensive and uncomfortable, feeling the strange wind was a bad omen for the voyage ahead.

Shortly after lunch the faint sound of a bugle informed all ears of the imminent arrival of the carts carrying the male prisoners. The Captain watched from the poop deck as the militia unfastened the men's chains and lined them up to board. There were no relatives or friends to see anyone off, the prisoners looking sullen and fatigued, those with small bags of personal belongings clutching them tightly.

The men's feelings ranged from total despair, through resignation, to faint hope that the new land may hold promise for a new life. Some were missing wives and children they knew they would probably never see again. Others were ill and dreading the sea voyage. Several were muttering prayers to themselves. One thing they all had in common was their unkempt look. Straggly beards, ragged hair, and sunken eyes were testament to hard times behind.

"Move on, ye landlubbers," the militia commander yelled. "The good life as you once knew it is over. For the rest of your days you scum will exist in hell. The worst will occur once you land in Botany Bay and line up in the chain gangs. But my intention is to ensure you are adequately prepared by introducing you to a new hell below decks. Welcome aboard, you filthy dregs of humanity."

Captain Fielding grimaced and muttered to himself, "I don't know about Botany Bay, but there'll be no hell on my ship if I can arrange it."

Chapter 12

"Prisoners, I am Captain Fielding, in command of this ship, the *Surrey*. We are going to be together in close quarters and proximity for several months. There are a number of rules for you to follow that will make life on board more tolerable for everyone. Those rules will be shared with you in a few moments. My job is to get you all safely to Botany Bay, so the worst thing any of you can do is impede my management of this ship. I make no judgment of your crimes. The militia have responsibility to ensure you receive the appropriate measures that our government has decreed. However, I will be closely overseeing the militia's role on my ship. The other man responsible for your well being is Dr. Jamieson. The ship will be leaving shortly on the ebb tide and will head for Portsmouth, where Dr. Jamieson will be replaced by Dr. Browning. The Surgeons' goal is to keep you all healthy throughout the voyage. I urge you to openly share your health concerns with Dr. Jamieson. All of you will be treated equally as much as that is possible. Food for women and men will be the same except for women pregnant or nursing. Exercise and access to facilities will be identical, punishment will be the same. I have no love of the whip and would welcome it staying unused.

"Rule number 1 is that cruelty to your fellow man will not be tolerated. You will use surnames to address each other, and there will be no name calling. You will be divided into 'messes' of about 6 persons each and elect a leader in each case. The leader will be responsible for ensuring equality of treatment for the members of his or her mess. A leader can be relieved of duty if all members of the mess complain.

"Rule number 2 is that you will attend divine services on Sundays. A number of Bibles will be supplied for your comfort. We will seek out teachers among you who will establish classrooms for those who can neither read nor write. This is a perfect chance to be educated.

"Rule number 3 concerns cleanliness. You will be living together in tight quarters. The militia will check on ventilation each morning. Do not close the scuttles, that is the portholes, unless ordered due to inclement weather. Your bedding must be brought topside once a week and brushed and aired. You will wash daily and you will wash your clothes weekly. You will sweep out your quarters weekly or more often if necessary. Mess leaders will organize a rotation of cleaners for the latrines. The cleaner you keep your quarters the more comfortable will be your voyage. Cockroaches, rodents, and lice should be eliminated with the help of our cat population, traps, molasses and other arrangements. No food should be left behind after meals. We are planning to stop at both Rio de Janeiro and Cape Town to replenish supplies of food and water, and make necessary repairs. I will be ordering the cooks to ensure your meals are as tasty and varied as they can make them.

"Now for rule number 4. I can do only so much as Captain. But I must remind you that you are prisoners of the government. Any attempt to escape or to cripple the ship's progress for such intention will be dealt with harshly. I might also point out that escape overboard in the middle of the Atlantic or Indian Oceans requires a very long swim home."

Mutterings of understanding, lots of nod heading, and even a little muted tittering ran through the crowd.

"One last point. The Surgeons and I have a responsibility to note any untoward behavior on the records we have to provide the authorities in New South Wales upon arrival. It behooves each and every one of you to do your best to comply with the rules and avoid any note against your name. I cannot undo the reasons you are aboard. I will try to make the journey bearable for all, but I cannot control Mother Nature, who will undoubtedly test us along the way.

"Would the Commander of the Militia guarding the men please step forward?"

No-one moved but the prisoners' heads turned as one to where the Commander was leaning against the second mast.

"I'll repeat my command. Come forward and be seen by everyone here, Sir."

Warily, the huge man in his tight red coat, saber dangling at his side, pushed through the crowd of prisoners and climbed up beside the Captain, who turned to address him. "I understand, Sir, from your speech on the wharf that it is your intention to make life totally miserable for the male prisoners. Did I hear you correctly?"

The Commander looked at the Captain, went as red in the face as his waistcoat and yelled so everyone could hear him, "These scum-faced dogs of criminals deserve nothing better, and that's how we will treat them. They are the pits of humanity and a disgrace to our society. We'll punish them to the maximum letter of the law for any infringement. It's my duty to do so."

"So my words to the prisoners a few moments ago meant nothing to you, apparently. I'm truly sorry to hear that. Let me clarify my position for your benefit and for the other members of the militia. There will be no untoward mistreatment of prisoners. On this ship they will be considered first as passengers, second as convicts, and except for totally unwarranted behavior, will be treated humanely.

"Quartermaster, take this man, gag him and tie him to the mast until we cast off. We will be leaving him behind."

Hearing this command, the Commander quickly reached for his saber, only to find the Captain pinning his arms to his side using his large matching bulk.

A cheer went up from the prisoners, half obliterating the Commander's yell to his compatriots: "Soldiers, draw your weapons and take charge."

The shouted command was to no avail, as Captain Fielding had planned well in advance with every intention of dealing publicly with the man. He'd anticipated the event by taking his officers aside and asking them to station two able-bodied seamen close by each soldier during his talk to the prisoners. Their instructions were to disarm the soldiers but not hurt them if occasion called for it. Now nine soldiers stood totally embarrassed as their leader was dragged by three sailors and tied to the main mast.

"Now, you remaining soldiers, which of you is in line to replace the Commander? One chap stepped forward. "That would be me, Sir."

"Good. You will all have your arms returned to you once we set sail, unless you feel kindred spirits with the Commander and would rather leave with him." No one moved.

"Congratulations and thank you.   Please continue with moving the male prisoners to their station below deck."

Dr. Jamieson stepped forward and whispered, "Very brave indeed, Captain. Congratulations. My respect for you has grown considerably. That was a brilliant tactical move.   In one stroke you have gained a large measure of respect with the prisoners and, perhaps more importantly, also with the crew. I doubt the Admirals and the military high command will love you when they learn, but by then you will be long gone.   I'd love to hear the Commander's report to his superiors."

The Captain had one more move in mind. He walked to the tied up soldier, and overlooking the venom in his scowl and the curses behind the gag, asked him, "Can you swim?   If so nod your head up and down."   Fear registered in the man's eyes as he interpreted the Captain's question as a threat to throw him overboard. He thrust his head and neck to and fro sideways in an obvious and desperate expression of inability.

"That's alright then, Commander. Frankly, I had no intention of pushing you overboard and leaving you to swim, as that would make me as common as you. I merely wanted you to experience a taste of the edge of that hell you promised the prisoners with your fear. You will be the last to leave the ship and probably should be prepared to jump the last foot or so to safety as the gangplank is pulled aboard."

He was pleased to see that the prisoner carts had gone and that the only men waiting on the dock were those who would release the thick rope lines from the giant bollards and cleats when the ship was ready to leave.

At 5:30 pm the Quartermaster untied the militia man and led him to the last rear gangplank as sailors stood by to haul it on board. There was a gap of two feet between its end and the dock and given a push the fellow was forced to run down the twin planks and jump.　He made it by inches and the dockhands jeered as he walked away.

The heavy lines were hauled on board and inch by inch the majestic barque slid away from its berth and headed east into the diminishing pale light over the European continent.

Dr. Jamieson watched as the Captain gave a series of sharp orders controlling the ship's graceful movement into the center of the Thames, and sighed heavily.　"A long way to go, Captain.　May the Gods of wind and sea be with you, and may you return home wealthier and wiser than now as you depart."

"Thank you, kind Sir.　Please join me in a sherry before dinner. I'm sure the crew can get us to Margate without our help.

"Beyond that to the south, who knows what challenges will test us."

Chapter 13

The sun shone, and the seas were amazingly calm for the first twenty four hours. Captain Fielding and the crew couldn't believe their good fortune. The whole contingent of prisoners, other than Molly Bridges in the onboard gaol, was allowed on deck as they passed the white cliffs of Dover, none of the men and women having seen them before. But as if in payback for the good deed, that evening the wind brought darkened, rain-filled clouds with it, and by midnight all the sails were furled and the ship hove-to as enormous gusts of horizontally driven rain pelted them from the west. For the passengers below deck with the hatches battened down and the scuttles closed, it was as if God was sending them a message castigating them for their sins. The ship rose and dove as monstrous waves slammed into the bow, and passengers held on to stanchions and each other as they were tossed from side to side. Children cried in fear and slid across the deck. And then the seasickness started to affect them one by one. There weren't enough pails to go around and those that were available soon filled with stinking vomit. The floor received the contents of stomach after stomach and soon the quarters were awash with ugly bile. Some adults gathered in a corner and prayed out loud for deliverance, others were too sick to care. Males and females were stricken equally. No one was spared nature's wrath.

The storm continued throughout the following day, and it wasn't until well beyond sundown before the ship was under way again and the hatches and scuttles were opened and fresh air flooded below deck. Mops and pails were passed down and large jugs of fresh water circulated amongst the ill. Dr. Jamieson wandered among the women offering seasickness medicine and treating a number of cuts and abrasions. He had managed to examine 30 more female passengers before the storm hit. Those of the remaining 37 who would make it to his rooms on the morrow would certainly have different complaints.

He arranged to have his gaol-bird released, finding her cowering and markedly sullen. "Have we gotten rid of all your spittle, Molly?" he said as he threw her clothes at her. "It's going to be a long journey. Better learn to behave now or you will spend a lot more time in confinement. Do you understand? Get out of my sight and let's see if the other women can stand you better than I can. Dismissed."

Back under deck, the male convicts were no better off than the women and seemed more reluctant to clean up after themselves. Dr. Jamieson called the mess leaders together, a number of whom had to send deputies, and gave them explicit instructions on how to proceed. Being more forward in the ship their quarters had sprung a number of small hull leaks so that their floor was miserably soupy, and cleanup took a lot longer than in the women's area. The Surgeon arranged for the leak holes to be stuffed with rags so marking the spots where the carpenter could effect repairs the following day.

Although the rain had passed, the seas were still heavy from the wind and slow progress was made along the coastline. Seasickness continued as the waves kept bouncing the ship up and down, rocking and rolling its frame at will. Few partook of food at lunch, and it was common for their neighbors to complain that the smell made their sickness worse.

It was a miserable period for all the convicts. As much as the Captain and Surgeon understood the situation there was little they could do. They both knew that the passengers had to go through the seasickness episode at some point, no matter what. The sooner they got past it, the better they'd be prepared for what lay ahead. Only 8 stalwart women made it to the doctor's quarters to be examined, and so he invited any men feeling strong enough, to also come forward. He abandoned seeing prisoners in alphabetical order and managed to see 12 men before dinner took him to the Captain's table.

"We should make Portsmouth day after tomorrow gentlemen, unless another infernal storm comes out of nowhere," the Captain said. "Tomorrow noon I want a detailed report of anything, above or below deck, that needs repair, replacement, or reinforcement. Each sail should be fully let out and checked for tears, ripped edges or holes that could become larger. And the rigging should be checked from top to bottom to ensure no strands of rope are working loose from being caught on a splinter of wood or anything metal. Commander, I imagine most of your men were seasick also. Are they coming around? Do any need Dr. Jamieson's ministrations? Are any still feeling mutinous over your predecessor's departure? Let me know if you get any sense of sustained ill-will, as we can arrange for replacements in Portsmouth."

The further west the ship traveled, the lighter the seas became and once beyond Eastbourne it was almost smooth sailing. By spending less time with each prisoner Dr. Jamieson managed to see 25 more women, two more pregnant in early stages. He'd examined 15 children ranging from a two month old girl to a 13 year old boy. One mother was having trouble producing enough milk for her child and he arranged for her to receive milk from the Captain's supply. In so doing he generated respect from the mothers on board, his compassion being greatly appreciated. He'd examined 6 of the supposedly 7 prostitutes on board, and given them dire warnings about being caught trying to entertain sailors, soldiers, or male convicts in return for rum or money. For those infected he provided medicine, fully cognizant however that his messages would likely be ignored. Only one, named Anne Mooney, seemed anxious to change her ways. On learning that at one stage she had been a teacher, he promised to mention her name to the Captain who planned to set up a small school on board.

As he examined more and more of the men he was disturbed to witness their physical condition. Most had spent time on one of the hulks – old ships no longer seaworthy that had been converted into floating prisons. These vessels housed between 800 and 1000 men in crowded conditions, worse than land gaols. Food was of poor quality and the men worked on shore helping build the infrastructure along the Thames, or in whatever port the hulk was anchored. Most of the men were disease free, which was remarkable in itself, but their strength was pathetic and their bodies skinny. Many had sunken eyes and sparse hair. Their ankles were often chafed where heavy chains had been applied. A number had open sores, and scars from whippings decorated far too many backs. He made a note to recommend increased bulk-building food and a regular exercise program for the men, perhaps led by a compassionate sailor.

As expected, there were a few with early symptoms of pneumonia, and, surprisingly, some with early indications of scurvy, having been denied sufficient citrus influence in their diet. Of the first 50 examined only one had syphilis. Married men were in a minority but many carried the extra burden of depression over being parted from their families. Formerly tough males would cry in the doctor's presence as they described the heartbreak of being torn away from wives and children. Family visitors to men on the hulks had been permitted on holidays, such as Easter and Christmas, but none of the men had had the chance to say any final goodbye when moved to the *Surrey.* The penal system in Britain was simply overwhelmed with numbers of so-called criminals, and extra, or special, considerations were few and far between. Women who had children with them in gaol brought them along, but no children accompanied the men.

The most able man was a single chap named George Farnborough, aged 23, who hailed from Newcastle on Tyne. He was a butcher who'd recently finished his apprenticeship. He had broad shoulders from carrying carcasses across his back and had somehow managed to preserve 95% of his size and strength. His story was a bit unusual in that he had given a small cooked piglet to a local church to be served in a meal for the poor and hungry. He made no pretense about it, but his master, while even appreciating the good deed, basically charged him with stealing from the shop's stock.

His trial took place within a week, at which the local minister and other adults provided positive character testimonials, but to no avail. He was convicted and sentenced to 7 years by a merciless judge whose only interest that day was to get trials completed as fast as possible. A local council official had connections with higher justice authorities, resulting in his being sent to the Middlesex gaol in London two days later, where he was added to the list of felons to be transported immediately. So, unlike essentially all the other men, he'd never been on a hulk and had spent only a few days in land gaols. He was still stunned by his master's decision to turn him in, having believed from previous conversations that the man would approve of his action. His bitterness caused him to no longer trust anyone.

Late on a calm afternoon the ship veered to starboard around Southsea and headed into the East Portsmouth Bay. The rattle of the anchor chain signaled to everyone that a few days' respite lay ahead.

Despite the initial information that had been shared with them, many of the convicts thought that the time spent between sea and land ports during the remainder of their voyage would be similar to what they had experienced so far.

The weeks ahead would reveal the magnitude of their mistaken hopes...

Chapter 14

Captain Fielding urged his officers and militia to watch for convicts who might feel compelled to try and escape with land so close at hand. He allowed the prisoners to be on deck together the next morning to get exercise and experience sunshine. He had minor repairs made to part of the deck railing, and replaced several of the shackles holding the rigging. As well, seven sails had their loose edges re-stitched.

Dr. Browning turned up shortly before noon, and immediately went over the passenger medical notes with Dr. Jamieson. Per his count there were still 4 women convicts to be examined, and 61 men. After dinner in the evening, the older doctor shook hands with the officers, wishing them well for the rest of the voyage. Captain Fielding raised a toast in his honor giving thanks for his contribution, and walked him to the cab waiting on the dock.

"You've established a good rapport with the convicts I talked to, Captain, both male and female. You are seen as an honest, hard-working man with great ingenuity and planning skills. The sailors respect you for your directness and support. I think you will find them a loyal crew. I can't imagine that you will see any mutinous behavior from them unless something drastic changes along the way.

"I do think that your naturally kind nature, coupled with your fairness, means you will be approached by certain women along the way with 'entertainment' in mind, maybe one or two possibly even looking for more long-lasting relationships.

My only advice is don't be hesitant in enjoying the perks of your position. You wouldn't be breaching any unwritten rules of society nor practices elsewhere in His Majesty's Navy.

"For now, however, I bid you adieu with grateful thanks for letting me come along on this part of the trip. It made an old heart young again. I certainly wish you a successful voyage. May the winds and waves be with you."

And with that he nodded to the driver, who closed the door, mounted the front seat and urged his horse out through the dock gates.

Repairs continued for a second straight day and the prisoners grew restless, even though they were allowed on deck again. While Dr. Browning continued the obligatory examinations, Captain Fielding watched with amusement as men and women intermingled, some pairing up shyly, and many women, clearly suspicious of male intent, making sure they stayed together in groups. Children beyond infant age were generally allowed to run free. When one bumped into a man, sometimes that fellow would use the occasion to seek out and start a conversation with the mother. All very normal, in the Captain's view.

On the morning ebb tide the *Surrey* hauled anchor and sailed south along the east coast of the Isle of Wight into the English Channel where she turned to starboard on a southwesterly course headed for the Celtic Sea. The winds were light so progress was slow, but at least it was fairly smooth sailing. Most of the prisoners came on deck to witness the last views of their homeland, staying there till the sun set and fading light hid the coastline. Tears filled many eyes, and at dinner the Captain had Dr. Browning hand out the twenty Bibles, which were eagerly taken up by the faithful.   In small groups some found solace in having portions read out loud – offsetting the sadness they felt at leaving the familiar world behind them.

Overnight they cleared English longitude and set course for Portuguese Madeira and thence to Spain's Canary Islands. In his examinations of 30 men yesterday, the doctor had come across two teachers, John Buckley, and Michael Keating, both of whom were willing to participate in onboard lessons for young boys and girls. In the main salon the Captain and the Surgeon sat with the two men and Anne Mooney, assessing their skills and subjects of particular interest. They looked through the list of 15 children's names Dr. Jamieson had provided, agreeing that the ten eldest could do with appropriate tutelage. On days when the sailing was smooth the children would gather in the salon for the hours between breakfast and lunch for classroom learning.   The subjects taught would include elementary introductions to writing, reading, arithmetic, composition, geography, and a little history.

From his special trunk the Captain retrieved the text-books plus fifteen chalkboards and two hundred chalk sticks. He had purchased the latter two items during the stop at Portsmouth when he realized there were no tools for students to use in the school he was planning. He wondered how he and Mrs. H. had overlooked such an obvious need. No matter. They were available now.

There were two things he worried a little about. First, would Anne Mooney be able to stay on the straight and narrow, and not inadvertently infect precious young minds with hints of immorality or make inappropriate approaches to the students. Indeed, would mothers be happy to have their children tutored by an ex-prostitute. To that end he arranged to have two teachers present at each sitting, where possible, ostensibly to teach different subjects to different age groups.

The second small concern was an expectation that a selected number of the adults who were totally illiterate or could only read, but not write, would also want schooling. He asked Dr. Browning to canvass the prisoners to gauge their level of interest.

The doctor finished examining the last 35 prisoners, most of whom were male, and on the following day he strolled among the women, seeking their input. For those mothers whose children would be in school, he handed out the fifteen children's books from the Captain's trunk, leaving them to sort out who would read which story to which children, and how they would share the books. The women were clearly impressed and very grateful for the Captain's gifts. He went up in their esteem yet again.

The information provided by the Admiralty to the Captain before sailing indicated that 23 women and 33 men were illiterate. The doctor found little enthusiasm among those women to learn more, with only two showing tentative interest, but was pleasantly surprised to find 12 men anxious to improve their lot, including 3 who were above 30 in age. The question became: who would be willing to teach them?

No answer came quickly, and the ship plowed on in front of the northeast trade winds and the Canary current. Each day at noon the Captain posted their position and the number of miles they had travelled in the previous 24 hours. The warm, calm weather, and better food than that served in the land gaols started to have an impact on the disposition of the prisoners. Dr. Browning and the militia contingent made sure discipline around cleanliness was followed, although there were natural grumblings by inmates forced to haul their mattresses to the deck and beat them. The mess leaders followed orders to keep the deck floor as clean as possible and worked hard at ridding their confines of rats and cockroaches. The population of the pests seemed to be dwindling, much to the relief of all.

Going over the notes on the women, the Surgeon identified 7 who had indicated they had skills as seamstresses. In a meeting in the main lounge the Captain had two sailors bring his trunk in, and to the delight of the women gathered, produced the bolts of cotton and woolen fabrics, skeins of wool and multiple accompanying sewing, and knitting accessories.

"Where we are headed, ladies, the temperature is only going to increase, so for now I think working with cotton would be most important. My desire is to make sure every girl and woman has decent coverage. I will leave it to you to establish the priorities amongst those in need but I anticipate that in the next few weeks I will see fewer and fewer rags worn as clothes than I see today. You do not need to create London fashions; patched dresses or new simple smocks will be adequate. We will use any discarded rags in the fire pits...."

A young woman interrupted… "Sir, if you would approve, Sir, I think we could use portions of the rags to make foot covers. As you've seen, many of the children and teenage girls are barefoot, and there are splinters in the decking.   The rags would not make shoes but if we have several thicknesses it could protect their feet better, Sir.   And if the deck gets hotter as we proceed it would also help prevent burning, Sir."

"That's an excellent idea. What else comes to mind, ladies?"

"Ah, Sir?   My specialty was making bonnets.   If there is enough material left over once we've made acceptable dresses for everyone I could make bonnets for the children. Especially the fairer ones, to help protect them from the sun and heat upside."

"Perfect, ladies. I'm showing you all the supplies here, but will keep anything woolen until later as I think you will be surprised how cold it will get before we reach Australia. Now, is there anything else you need at the moment?"

A chorus of "No, Sirs" and "Thank you, Sirs" filled the room as the women smiled and picked up the supplies and hurried out. Their smiles warmed the Captain's heart. 'No, Sir,' he thought. 'No hell on my ship.' An image of Mrs. Hutchinson sorting through patterns back in the drapery shops flitted in and out of his mind. 'Thank you, good lady. If only you could see how happy you've made these women. It is you they owe, not me.' …

Chapter 15

Anne marked another day on the calendar hanging on the back of the kitchen door. She counted again. 18 days the Captain had been gone, 11 days since he'd sent the note from Portsmouth. 'Such a thoughtful man to write back to his housekeeper,' she thought. 'Maybe I should really think of myself as his 'mistress.' not 'housekeeper.' After all I have fulfilled a certain function mistresses provide, and he does pay me to look after him. Do mistresses pay bills and clean their providers' houses, I wonder? Oh dear, if I miss him this much already, how will I handle the months ahead?'

She pulled out his note from her apron pocket and read it for the tenth time.

"Dear Mrs. H.,

Well, we are on our way and are now anchored in Portsmouth. We encountered a very fierce storm west of Dover which created minor damage, mostly to our sails, and which caused a great deal of seasickness amongst our passengers. I'm pleased to say that they now seem to be better, but we've a long way to go and there's bound to be more serious storms ahead, I imagine.

Dr. Browning will be replacing Dr. Jamieson tomorrow. The good old doctor did an admiral job for us, establishing good discipline below deck. A lot of the male prisoners still are to be examined, but there are no major surprises. We have 4 pregnant women, two well advanced, two not quite showing. And I'm delighted to report that one of the young prostitutes is committed to turning over a new leaf and helping teach the young children. I hope she might present an example to the other ladies of the night.

I dismissed the militia commander at the docks in London as he seemed to be of the wrong character to be in charge of the prisoners. The remaining militia guards seem competent, but I am sure I will have my hands slapped by the Admiralty for my decision once I return. So be it. I've yet to share any of the good things in my special trunk, but as soon as we leave here I will distribute the Bibles. I have a feeling they may provide nice comfort as the shores of England fade from view.

I'm actually looking forward to sharing the extra personal supplies you helped me buy. I am sure they will give the prisoners some joy in their horrid world, and of course whenever the trunk is opened I will be reminded of you. The cooks do their best but cannot match your tasty dinners.

I hope you are keeping well.

With sincere regard, I remain your loyal friend

Captain Fielding"

Perhaps a little formal at the end, but what did she expect? Love and kisses? Definitely not the Captain's style. And at least he had been thoughtful enough to write. Most men with housekeepers simply took them for granted from what she had heard. Ordered them around as if they were chattel, and then took advantage of them sexually whenever the urge arose. Of course, she reflected, she wouldn't mind a little more physical attention, as she was still young at heart, and spritely and healthy for her age. But the Captain treated her like a lady and that was far better than being regarded as a servant or slave.

The Portsmouth postmark on the Captain's letter brought back memories of times and scenes in her life before she came to London. Aside from her parents she'd lost three other meaningful people in the two naval towns she had lived in. Her husband in Plymouth had abused her but died in an accident that spared her extended humiliation and hurt. In hindsight it was easy to tell herself she should have been stronger and left the marriage voluntarily much earlier. Her sister Eliza had seen through William but Anne had been blinded by his charisma and earnest promises. She was indebted to Eliza who rescued her and brought her to Portsmouth when William had died and her finances had run dry. The two women had lived together many years before Eliza died of consumption 4 years ago. Anne was lucky she never fell ill.

But the real ache in her heart was for her son Edward. Unable to stand up against his father's brutish behavior, he had simply walked away from home that fateful day, and had joined the miners in the nearest coal mine to town. Over the intervening three years before William died she'd tried to visit him on several occasions but Edward had deliberately avoided her. She worried about the trials and conditions he had to suffer through as a pit boy at the lowest rungs of cheap labor exploited by the mine owners.

Her memory was haunted by the final glimpse she had of him from her last visit. As she climbed the path uphill from the mine and turned to look back, he had come out from behind a building where he had been hiding, and stood silently watching her. His clothes and face and arms were covered in black soot, but he lifted his cap as if in salute to tell her he was OK. She waved back, but he turned and headed for the mine entrance, leaving her wondering if she'd ever see him again.

He'd be twenty six years old now, she realized. Was he still at the mine she wondered or had he moved on? Or worse, had his lungs been damaged like those of many of the other miners, and he was now an invalid somewhere, or worse, had succumbed to a miserable death. She wished she knew more, but she had no desire to head back to Plympton to try and find out. Too many years had passed, and as much as it wrenched her heart when the memories came flooding in, she resigned herself to never knowing his fate for sure.

In a way, she told herself, she was like some of the women convicts on board the Captain's ship. While a number were able to bring a child with them, no doubt many had had to leave family behind and would never see any of them again. Parish churches or relatives would raise them, many of the latter resentful at having to feed yet another mouth. How well would such extra burdens be treated?

The kettle's whistle brought her out of her musings, and she poured the hot water into the teapot, only half-filling it, given the Captain's absence. She'd made his favorite scones again today and indulged unashamedly in the thick cream and jam she applied liberally to the halves.

'He should be nearing Madeira soon,' she thought. Three years back the Captain had bought one of the new paper-lined globes, but as more precise geography of current and new countries around the world was realized, especially in the southern Pacific Ocean, the globe was soon out of date and it had been relegated to a dusty corner in the attic. Still, she remembered some of the country representations they had looked at together. One day she thought, globes will probably be standard educational tools for students to learn about geography. For now they were more novelty than anything else.

Even so, her intuition about Madeira was spot on. ...

Chapter 16

The island of Madeira was astern by about 5 miles when the lookout first spotted the massive dark cloud creeping up behind them. It stretched at least two miles across by his reckoning and was clearly gaining on the ship. Not knowing what wind strength it might be holding, Captain Fielding had most of the sails furled, slowing the boat and allowing the cloud to approach faster. It was a deep grey in color, the center perhaps 700 or 800 yards off the port side. At about a half mile back it released its first curtain of showers, reducing visibility and gently frothing the sea. With the officers watching and assessing, the consensus was that this was a light squall that would provide not much more than a wash of the decks, rigging and masts, and replenish the water barrels.

It was 2 pm in the afternoon, and directly above, the sun was still bearing down with its summer intensity. Clearly soon to be extinguished as the rain caught up with them. The Captain drew his Surgeon aside and they chatted briefly. Then, in response to a sailor's command to batten down the hatches, said "Hold it, seaman. This may be a good opportunity to let the prisoners get a real cleansing courtesy of mother nature. Guards, tell them the situation and invite them to come topside with any clothes to wash. The Surgeon has gone to get extra soap and brushes and combs. Stand by and watch that no one slips under the railing or falls into the cannon when the deck gets slippery. I think they may welcome this opportunity."

Within 15 minutes the deck fore and aft was filled with folks anxious to wash themselves and their spare clothes. They watched as the edge of the cloud started to blot out the sun and drop the temperature a few degrees. Then suddenly they were all soaking wet as the deluge arrived. Exuberant shouts filled the air, and it wasn't long before men's shirts and pants were coming off and being waved jubilantly. Not to be outdone, a few of the less bashful women also slipped out of their chemises and uniforms, and bars of soap passed from hand to hand as backs were scrubbed and women's hair untangled and combed. Eventually the deck was full of naked prisoners, happy to be showered upon, heedless of the spectacle they provided to one another. For most of the male guards and sailors, voyeurism was all the entertainment they needed, although several sailors not on active duty quickly joined in the melee.

The rain lasted twenty five minutes, and gradually lessened to small drips which the wind soon dispensed. The sun appeared behind the rear edge of the cloud and immediately steam began to rise from the wet bodies. Everyone relished the chance to dry off and hang their clothes over stanchions and rails and on any loose rigging to pick up both wind and heat. Men and women converged in small groups to discuss animatedly the common experience they had just enjoyed. Lustful male eyes were obvious, but most of the women seemed not to care, although the ladies of the night watched carefully for prolonged interest, and marked targets in their minds for later approaches.

While the convicts were on deck, the Captain made a surreptitious tour of their quarters. He noticed minor flooding through cracks in the ceiling as rainwater sloshed across the deck planks topside, but otherwise he was pleased at the general cleanliness and the ingenuity some prisoners exhibited in making their stations more comfortable or convenient. Satisfied, he returned to his cabin via a stern hatchway, hardly getting wet.

He took off his hat, shook the water off it, and hung it on the peg behind the door. Halfway through unbuttoning his jacket a soft voice made him turn toward his bed in the alcove. "Well, I thought you were never coming back, Captain. You look flushed. Why don't you lock the door and join me here. That shower has washed me all over and I'm so nice and clean."

A young nubile girl with braided hair lifted the blanket revealing her nude form gracefully adorning the undersheet. No question she was very pretty, her face pixie-like, her handful-sized breasts standing out firmly and her pubic hair slicked down framing her bulging pudenda.

"My name is Margaret Ebbit, and I'd love to be your companion for a while. Friends call me Maggie."

"Perhaps I will indulge, Maggie. I'm impressed you made it here undetected."

"Well... I did have to offer a small bribe to one of the seamen, Sir, who saw me in the corridor. I think he might keep his satisfaction to himself for now though."

"Where are you from, Maggie?" the Captain asked as he stepped out of his remaining clothes.

"Oh, here and there, Cap'n. Mainly around London. I'm a minister's daughter. Learnt a lot from the way father looked after a few of the better-looking penniless lady parishioners."

"No mother around?"

"Don't think she could stand the competition. Left before I was ten years old." A pause, then…. "Now, can we stop talking and share this space together? I'm sure you'll have to be back on deck sometime."

'Sometime' didn't occur for another two hours, as the Captain proved the flesh is weak and willing and Maggie added another scalp to her mental belt of trophies. "Can't do much better than this one," she told herself after quaffing the glass of rum the Captain offered as 'payment for services rendered.'

"Well, I am on the High Seas, a long way from home," the Captain told himself. "Why should I stay lonely purely because Mrs. Hutchinson elects to… I'll keep it as discreet as possible."

No more rain followed the one major episode and with another two days' sailing they spotted Tenerife ten miles off to starboard. The northeasterly trade winds shifted a little more to the east and the Captain steered for the coast of South America. The temperature started to rise more rapidly, gaining almost a full degree every day.

Fishing for dolphins became the pastime 'du jour' for off-duty sailors, with several being caught and providing fresh but tough meat which was not universally enjoyed. The much smaller bonito fish were tastier and easier to catch. Fresh fish caught by sailors was shared with the crew first and only if there was enough left over did the prisoners get any. When free to exercise on deck, the prisoners became enthusiastic supporters of those crew fishing, urging them to bring in multiple catches so they may have fresh meat too.

One day a remarkable phenomenon occurred; flying fish leapt out of the water and landed directly on deck. The sailors yelled with mirth as flying fish flew across the deck in huge numbers. Some hit the seamen directly. Others simply landed on the deck. Pails were quickly gathered and fish loaded into them. The 'shower' went on for fifteen minutes, at the end of which there were twenty five pails of fresh food taken to the cooks. A few of the crew had seen it before but neither the Captain nor Surgeon had. Once again the prisoners dined well.

As the boat approached the equator the heat started to get to everyone. Even more so as the following wind died down in strength. Even in the shadow of the sails the temperature rose to 90 degrees and the floor boards of the deck were too hot to stand on for long. Men were appearing shirtless and in pants cut down to shorts while women wore sleeveless chemises and short skirts. The idea was for adults to wear only as much as minimal decency required. Children however wore their cotton smocks, hessian footwear and protective bonnets.

As the temperature rose and the ship traveled fewer and fewer miles each day, tempers flared and discomfort increased for everyone. As well, the cockroaches grew greatly in number, as with the increased heat their breeding process seemed to speed up. How the prisoner population longed for another rain-filled storm! But it wasn't to be. For four days the ship actually was becalmed just north of the equator. Not a breath of air circulated through the sails, which hung limply from the spars. It was at this point that the Captain decided to break out the board games he had acquired to give the convicts something new to fill their vacant hours.

Even the simple game of checkers was a big hit, perhaps because it wasn't really that hard to play and anyone could learn fast. It took a little more skill to play peg solitaire and the game of the goose, but soon there were waiting queues for access to all the boards. Once again the Captain scored points for his kindness and consideration. The elegant chess set he had bought, however, stayed in his cabin.

The sailors had three main forms of self-entertainment. One involved contests of arm-wrestling. The other two involved races, seeing who could climb the rigging fastest; and swimming. Many more men competed in the latter races, since they got relief from the heat in the water. There were two favorite types of swimming contests. The first involved swimming around the ship, with two men diving off the stern in opposite directions and swimming alongside the respective hulls. Prisoners ran from side to side to check progress, and someone was always at the bow to see which swimmer got there first before heading back on the other side. There was great merriment and cheering as heat after heat progressed, and the eventual winner received an extra share of grog and accolades from his mates.

A second swim race involved long distance competition. Six participants would be rowed out in a long boat about half a mile off the beam. They would dive in together and race back to the stern of the ship. A shouted commentary from a sailor high in the rigging would give spectators information on who was leading, as sometimes with the swells it was hard to see from the ship's rail how the heads were aligned in the water. The passengers became enthusiastic supporters of select seamen and applauded their efforts no matter who came first.

By the fourth day becalmed however the attempts at self-entertainment by crew, militia and prisoners alike were half-hearted. The heat was too intense. The easiest relief for the prisoners was simply to lie still in their bunks, fanning themselves, or trying to sleep. Conditions were utterly miserable and the Captain could do nothing about it but wait.

A pounding on the Captain's door at 2 am in the morning brought him quickly topside where sailors were celebrating the tiniest breeze that was barely puffing the sails. But the ship was definitely moving, at no more than 2 knots, although it felt faster given their stationary position of the previous days. The breeze was from the northwest, and the Captain decided to let it blow them where it wanted as opposed to sticking to a southwesterly course aimed for the coast of South America.

Later when the prisoners woke they were ten miles closer to the equator and the first major marking point of their journey.

Chapter 17

While the prisoners were topside for their morning exercises, a tall black Satan-like figure rushed across the deck with a letter to the Captain from Neptune announcing his intention of coming on board with his suite the next day. The favor of a reply was requested, so the Captain sent word back with the runner that he'd be pleased to entertain the visitors. In a spirit of curiosity the prisoners asked the messenger to read the letter sent to the Captain out loud, which he did:

> Palace of Chrystal
> Sir,
> I have the honour of informing you and also my Children that you have been brought here to this glorious place. I shall come on board tomorrow in company with her Majesty Amphitrite and all those that are necessary in the duty of crossing the Equinox.
> I shall therefore mention the principal characters that will do their duty. The celebrated Dr. Sea Water who is supplied with pills, drops, etc. likewise Mr. Sharp Edge the Barber who has attended her Majesty for the last Three hundred years. He has been the last Three Months sharpening his razor which is now ready for action.
> I am
> Your Obedient Servant
> Neptune.
>
> P.S. I will also bring Her Majesty's Hair-dresser who dressed Ladies Hair in the first fashion.

The next day the prisoners gathered to witness the ceremony recognizing sailors who were crossing the equator for the first time. Smiles lit their faces as Neptune and Amphitrite with their followers came forward and invited the 'gentlemen' to be shaved, which they were obliged to submit to.

Many of the men had full beards from a month at sea and more and were apprehensive about the shaving process. A sail was filled with water and the 'patient' sat on the edge. Neptune welcomed him to the Southern Hemisphere and shaved him with a piece of old iron. As the man gasped for breath they tipped him head over heels into the sail, Neptune's followers holding his head down in baptism. The spectators applauded as the poor chap sputtered in misery. But after watching several men suffer this way, the tables were suddenly turned as unseen sailors in the rigging tipped pails of water over the prisoners below, soaking them through. That way they too were welcomed to the Southern Hemisphere by Neptune and Amphitrite.

The Captain came forth and thanked everyone for participating and offered Rum to sailors, militia and prisoners alike. The cooks had prepared scones as a treat and these too were shared. The whole occasion turned into one of merriment and laughter, bringing a little humanity to the uncomfortably wet passengers. With shrewd eyes the Surgeon and Captain watched several couples retreat to less conspicuous spots on deck to share their meals and stories, some unabashedly cuddling and fondling, enjoying each other's company. The Captain noted "Some of those relationships will want to become permanent before we reach Botany Bay, doctor. Mark my words."

"Aye Sir, I'm sure of it. And I must say I'm in favor. Most of these people are regular citizens caught trying to feed themselves to stay alive. They don't deserve to be sent to this ridiculous penal colony on the other side of the world. Anything that can make life more normal for them while we travel I endorse. I like what you've done so far, Sir. You are a true gentleman and I'm proud to serve alongside you."

"I thank you, Dr. Browning, for your support. The limited number of prisoners I have talked to seem as ordinary as many of my acquaintances and neighbors. And I must say, as the women put on a little weight, wear better clothes, and keep clean, some are appearing quite attractive. Even the men are starting to look better, gauntness is gradually disappearing from their frames, and they are starting to look after themselves, especially their hair. I'm sure I have you to thank for that."

"I've been reluctant to give them a razor that might be used to trim beards, in case someone used it for fighting. But given Neptune's treatment of the sailors I'm thinking of setting up a barber shop on deck one day and having the men who want it to volunteer for beard removal at the hands of experienced barbers, of which we have two on board."

"That's a great idea, doctor. It would help them tolerate the heat as well. Make sure the two barbers are rewarded appropriately with grog. They'll deserve it. Is there anything more we need to do for the women?"

"For one in particular, yes. Sarah Killeen, who is 26, should deliver any day. The heat has been terribly hard on her and I truly worry about her baby surviving. I suspect we'll need to augment her milk supply, and as well, we may need to create a movable perch that can be placed under the shadow of a sail so the baby can get the benefit of any breeze, no matter what direction it comes from. You may not be aware, Captain, but the heat in the prisoners' quarters is absolutely stifling and the men and women go about naked down there these days. They put minimal clothes on to come on deck. I understand that certain men engage in illicit relations with one another but am powerless to stop them. The women seem better behaved, although when it was cooler I know a couple of the prostitutes were in the men's quarters offering varied services. There seems to be a tolerance through the lower deck to not complain about extra-curricular behavior. Unless it gets out of hand or interferes with other necessary activity I'm not going to make a fuss. It's possible things may change once we get out of this tropical heat, of course."

"I'm happy to leave that in your capable hands and at your discretion, doctor. Do let me know about Miss Killeen though. We'll do what we can for her and her baby."

Two days sailing south of the equator brought a cry from the forward lookout. His "Ship ahoy," brought all the officers on deck and raised telescopes to several eyes. Ten miles away but coming towards them, in full sail, it was hard to identify exactly what flag it was flying. Guesses abounded until the consensus as she came closer made her to be a British freighter making good speed. The ships closed and hove-to with a hundred yards separating them.

The Captain sent the Surgeon and two of his officers with a rowing crew across the waters to exchange greetings. The

'Salisbury' was on its way from Rio to London with a load of timber, gold, and diamonds. Captain Gainsborough and three officers came back to the "Surrey' in their own boat and joined the Captain in the main salon and lounge, where experiences and voyage histories were eagerly shared. Rio's economy and the Brazilian colony as a whole was apparently in disarray because of the decline of mine output and price competition from Central America for the world sugar market. The value of exports from Rio's port was almost half of what it had been 50 years earlier. There was hope that coffee production and the resettlement of the Portuguese royal family in Brazil would turn things around, but the economy was currently in an unstable condition.

The news was disquieting, as the *Surrey* had planned to stop in Rio to replenish supplies. Given the situation there, the fact that the ship was not as far westward at the equator as the Captain had originally wanted, and that they had been becalmed so long, he decided to head directly for Cape Town instead. Having only encountered a couple of storms to date, there were still animals available for ham and mutton and even hens for eggs and chicken meat if needed. Drinking water was probably the main concern, but it was hardly likely that they'd make Cape Town, at least a month away, without encountering another storm or two.

They asked Captain Gainsborough if he could wait another thirty minutes while officers dashed off letters for loved ones back home, and as thanks they offered him and his men a shark they had caught the previous evening. Captain Fieldming wrote briefly:

Dear Mrs. H.,

We crossed the equator a few days ago and Neptune came to visit the crew. We had a merry time. We needed it after being becalmed for four days north of the line in heat over 90 degrees. It has adversely affected crew, militia and prisoners alike. We were originally planning to visit Rio but due to economic instability there we are going to head directly to Cape Town from here instead. The 'Salisbury', out of Rio, is carrying our letters home. This is the first ship we have encountered since leaving the continent behind.

The bolts of cotton you chose have been put to great use in smocks and bonnets and the board games provided the major relief during the heat. Always when I go to my trunk I am reminded of your goodness. The 'Salisbury' is patiently waiting for our mail so thank you once again for helping make this voyage more acceptable than it would have been otherwise. I will write again from Cape Town.

Please stay well.

With sincere regard, your loyal friend

Captain Fielding

Firing one cannon in a mock goodbye salute the *Surrey* turned south east and the two ships moved apart.

The steamy tropical heat sustained itself for the next three days, and as Dr. Browning had anticipated, Sarah Killeen gave birth to a baby boy shortly after the *Salisbury* departed. His skin was more red than pink, and his cries harsher than a normal baby's. Cool damp cloths were regularly spread across his body, and supplemental milk was provided by the cooks. Other mothers got involved by taking him on deck to feel whatever breeze existed as the ship tacked across the wind.

Despite all the care and attention however the little fellow did not fare well in the oppressive heat and refused to take milk as his skin dried. The Surgeon did what he could to support him, but to everyone's sadness and dismay, the boy died in his mother's arms late one evening. It was hard for everyone to come to grips with the loss. Sarah had carried him through her incarceration in the Middlesex gaol, and then on board, desperately longing to give life to her most precious possession, only to see him come and go in less than three days. What greater cruelty could befall her? Was this the ultimate punishment for her crime? Was God getting even twice – sending her thousands of miles away from her family, and then denying her the most important reminder of the life she was leaving behind? There were many women who didn't want children but bore them anyway. Why couldn't he have taken one of them instead of hers which she had wanted and loved so much? Life was totally unfair. Her tears seemed endless and the other mothers understood and empathized. Trying to provide comfort was difficult, as there were no adequate words to mitigate her loss.

To make matters worse, the mother had to suffer through the funeral service the next morning. A small gathering of sympathetic crew and convict friends stood at the ship's rail where the Captain led the service. The church service pennant was raised to the top of the forward mast and the little boy was wrapped in his blanket and heavy canvas. Weights were attached to his feet, and he was laid on a plank suspended at the rail. The captain spoke compassionate words to Sarah, recognizing her sorrow, devastation, and sense of helplessness, then read a psalm of comfort. He asked Sarah to step forward and state the name of her son out loud for everyone to hear. He then intoned, "We therefore commit this child's body to the deep, to be turned into corruption, looking for the resurrection of the body when the sea shall give up her dead, and the life of the world to come, through our Lord Jesus Christ; who at his coming shall change our vile body, that it may be like his glorious body, according to the mighty working whereby he is able to subdue all things unto himself."

At this point the Surgeon tilted the plank, and the little body slid gently into the sea.

After the Lord's Prayer and the Benediction, the captain attempted to console the distraught mother with kind words, but nothing could really shake the despair she now felt. The small set of friends crowded around in support, but there was little they could offer. Sarah had no other children, and for the moment there was only a gnawing emptiness. One second her son was still with her, in the next he was gone. Gone to a grave with no headstone, in a place never to be revisited. His winsome little features would exist only in memories.

A somber mood fell across the whole ship, and stayed throughout the day. There were desultory attempts to play games but no one's heart was really in it. People conversed in low tones in small groups, with heads hung, tears in many eyes. The prisoners had become a caring community in the weeks at sea and this tragedy was a startling reminder of the frailty of life in their current environment. The heat didn't help.

As if to add insult to injury, a massive squall moved in after dinner with thunder and lightning. Many who were superstitious felt God was angry at losing a life and was sending down punishment. Huddled downstairs they felt the wind pick up and rock the boat more violently than they remembered in the first storm. The squall turned into an intense gale, building 20 ft. seas in front of 50 mph gusts. The Captain could do little but ride with the wind, backing up on the miles they had progressed the past day or so. Even dragging the anchor had little effect, and the crew's main concern was to ensure the rigging stayed as taut as possible, holding the masts sturdy.

The storm continued through the next day with no lessening in its fury. Rain soaked the crew and created leaks in the deck planking as loose items were flung around. No meals were sent below and the prisoners were bounced from one position to another mercilessly. Some were seasick again, adding to the general misery. Blind to the size of the waves, they could only guess at the timing of troughs and swells, and try to anticipate them, but Mother Nature was not predictable in the South Atlantic and she caused more and more bruises as the hours dragged on.

When the storm finally passed, the ship had lost nearly 60 miles, which they slowly recovered through expert sailing. A passing comment to Dr. Browning made by one of the mothers who had been friendly with Sarah Killeen led the Surgeon to chat with her about teaching reading and writing to the adults on board. She had been a middle school teacher but didn't volunteer before due to her pregnancy. Now she was more receptive to the idea, and the Surgeon and others felt it would be a good way to distract her and give her something new to occupy her time and attention, rather than continually mourning the loss of her baby.

A magical change was felt by all 8 days on when the wind suddenly shifted direction markedly. At roughly 30 degrees south of the equator they had suddenly picked up the heavy westerlies and now speed rose dramatically. They turned from a southerly tack to a full blown wind-assisted south easterly direction aiming directly for Cape Town. Cheers went up each noon when the Captain posted the mileage of the previous twenty four hours – 105 miles, 120, 145, 150, even a 210 showed up one day. The extra speed plus the drop in temperature made everyone feel markedly better, even though it remained near 80 degrees in the shade of the sails.

Even so, restlessness among the prisoners still showed as they realized they were only halfway through their journey. Both men and women were frustrated with sexual desire, especially since they were quartered within each other's earshot. Encouraged by several pairs, some of the men got creative and strung ropes across the ceiling at one end of their quarters, and hung blankets to make 4 semi-secluded areas which became well-accepted spots for coupling when their needs could not be ignored. The cooler weather also revived the spirits and interests of three of the known prostitutes, who ignored the male convicts and concentrated on the sailors, other crew members including the cooks and the carpenter, and the guards.

An unfortunate incident befell one of the night ladies, however. Early one morning her soft whimpers led to her being discovered shoved under a heavy canvas cover in one of the longboats, severely beaten. She was rushed to the Surgeon's rooms in heavy distress, semi-conscious and breathing irregularly. Her face was covered in contusions and one eye was swollen closed. She had marks around her throat and her hair was in total disarray. Her left arm was broken, and two fingers on her right hand were bent back at an awkward angle. Her chemise had been ripped and deep scratches ran down between her breasts. A clear bite mark was on one of them. A mop handle was lying between her legs and she was oozing blood. At first the Surgeon wasn't sure she'd last out the day given the extent of her injuries, but she was tougher than her assailant had predicted, and once the doctor had gotten her breathing evened out and a sip of brandy inside her, color started returning to her face and she was able to utter a few words, although still not fully conscious.

Her attacker had had sex with her near one of the masts but had gotten violent once she told him no more and demanded payment. That's where he started punching her in the face and abdomen. At one point he grabbed her arm and dashed it ferociously against the mast which is when the bone snapped. She fell to the deck and he bent down and broke her two fingers. She thought she passed out from the pain but vaguely remembers him using the mop on her before picking her up and throwing her into the longboat. She'd have no trouble identifying him, she said.

The Surgeon called the Captain in and described what he learned. They gave the woman more brandy until she fell back fully asleep. The Surgeon decided to manipulate her broken arm back into position since she was half unconscious and would feel less pain with the alcohol she'd absorbed. His experience paid off and with only a mild grunt from her, he reset her bone. Two boards were used as a splint and bound with strong canvas to keep them in place. He bathed and cleaned her cuts and checked her internally, relieved to find no fresh bleeding. Cold cloths placed on her face helped to reduce the swelling, although the fact that her injuries had occurred many hours before would limit their impact. The men placed her on a hospital bed covering her with a light blanket.

The Captain assembled all the able bodied seamen on deck, and addressed them sternly.   "Last night a woman prisoner was beaten severely and left to die in one of the longboats. However she will recover thanks to the Surgeon's medical prowess.   I have been tolerant of your interaction with members of the opposite sex, but I will not stand for violence against them. Someone amongst you has perpetrated this indecent crime and will be punished as an example to others. We are halfway through this trip and I mean to see that the remainder is free from any such repeated behavior. If the man is among you now, he should step forward. Otherwise the victim will pick him out later."

A voice from the back yelled, "It was Blount, Sir. He's in his bunk dead drunk."

The Captain turned to the militia commander. "Go retrieve the miserable cur and lock him in the prison. Then come to my office to discuss punishment. We need to establish the appropriate response. Ok men, you are dismissed."

Chapter 18

As much as the Captain detested corporal punishment, the severity of Richard Blount's attack on the convict woman definitely deserved a whipping. He was made to 'strip to the gun' whereby he had to unbutton his lower garments and lie across a cannon where he received at short intervals thirty lashes with the 'cat' on his bare back and behind. He screamed in agony but the attendant crowd had little sympathy on learning the extent of their neighbor's wounds. The Surgeon checked him over, then had him placed back in the prison with a diet of bread and water. The militia were put in charge of his disposition with plans to turn him over to civil authorities in Cape Town.

The young woman stayed in the hospital for two days, in shock and pain. Her profession was known to be dangerous, but even so, none of her fellow ladies of the night had expected such violence on board the ship. Their trust, always on edge, was shaken to the core, and for two weeks afterwards they stayed in their quarters, away from the crew and guards.

The temperature stabilized in the mid seventies and the ship fairly sped across the waves. One day they averaged 10 knots and managed 240 miles, a record speed for the Captain and for the ship. Both the Captain and the Surgeon received clandestine visits from Maggie, neither man shying from engagement with her. Word spread and the Surgeon especially started to receive more female visitors to his rooms with feeble requests for treatment of made-up complaints. Since the death of his wife he'd never had so much attention, and he found he was not as old as he had mentally considered himself, able to satisfy younger women quite adequately.

Ruth Wickham, aged 31, had an extra degree of maturity that definitely appealed. She'd been widowed five years earlier when her husband had died of pneumonia after a protracted illness. The couple had no children despite years of trying. For the years she was single she had lived by her wits, often taking on menial jobs to keep herself going. She had an engaging personality, good looks, and a hard-work ethic. Good references helped her get better and better jobs, but as a maid to a well-off family she made a mistake of alienating a footman who eventually moved an expensive silver vase to her room which was discovered, and caused her expulsion. She vowed to get even but never got the chance. Life spiraled down after that until she was apprehended for stealing coins from the money drawer in the pub where she worked in order to generate a little savings. She'd been in gaol for six months before she was chosen for transportation.

She actually had a nasty cough when she first took herself to Dr. Browning's rooms, but they found unusual common ground when it turned out that he knew the well-to-do family that had dismissed her. Not that he could do anything to redress the situation, but he and the gentleman owner had once belonged to the same club in London before Dr. Browning and his wife moved to Portsmouth permanently. That was well before Ruth had been an employee of the man.

She blushed admitting she'd offered her body on occasion to a guard in order to be in a cell by herself and to receive better food. It was survival time, and with her feminine wiles she'd managed to retain her health and good looks while others deteriorated. It was a great relief however when she heard she was to be transported, recognizing that this would be her best opportunity to start a new life. She was not scared about finding her way in an unknown land.

Her story was not that unique, but her reasoned approach to life and her optimistic outlook captured the good doctor's interest. He checked the notes made by his predecessor who had also noted her realistic attitude. Dr. Jamieson's intimate examination had found no signs of infection but in fact a more healthy body than most of the women had.

With appropriate treatment Ruth's cough disappeared in two weeks, and she and the Surgeon found themselves seeking each other's company whenever they were on deck together. They were standing at the bow one day when the lookout not far above them yelled and pointed out a large bird flying across the ship's path.

An albatross! Soon there were six of them and the passengers scrambled to deck to see them. Their presence meant only one thing—they were getting closer to land. Albatrosses had a unique way of flying that was highly efficient in the air, using special soaring techniques to cover great distances with little exertion. They fed on fish and squid by surface seizing or diving. Two of the militia got lines to catch the albatrosses with a hook and bait in the form of pork fat. A piece of wood was tied about a foot from the bait to keep it near the water surface and it was hoped the albatrosses would swoop down and get snagged.

Simultaneously, more enterprising sailors rigged a line aloft and hung ropes with hooks through the bait at the end. Two albatrosses were caught this way as they swirled through the air and swallowed the pork. Down on deck the prisoners were surprised to see how large the birds were—one with a wing span more than twelve feet across. The sailors and officers were rewarded with albatross pie a day later. The cooks explained how they made the pies. First they steeped the birds in salt water overnight. They then boiled them in new salt water, and then boiled them again in fresh water with vinegar added. The large birds had a lot of meat and the final process was to bake the meat with salt, pepper, and vinegar to remove any fishy taste. The officers declared their meal delicious, and the convicts listened to their praise with envy. One of the more experienced sailors leathered the feet of one of the birds and made them into excellent tobacco pouches. He kept one and sold the other to a teammate.

From that day on everyone got more interested in miles covered, speed and estimated distance to the coast of South Africa. When "Land ho" finally sounded from the lookout on high, the prisoners rejoiced, hugging each other, smiling, clambering to the rails looking for the smudge of brown on the horizon that spelled stoppage and short-term relief from the vagaries of the ocean voyage.

They'd survived a horrendous journey and were nearly two thirds of the way to Botany Bay. The rest of the journey should be no trouble at all.

Famous last words.

Chapter 19

The anchor chain made its wonderfully distinctive rattling sound as it descended to the harbor floor, and the ship swung around it, facing into the wind. New sounds reached the ears of the prisoners, all of whom were on deck with the Captain's permission. The sun was shining, haloing the city, with Table Mountain rising majestically above the multitude of odd-sized buildings. A simple wooden jetty reached out into the bay, and a large number of rowboats plied back and forth between the jetty and various schooners and barques, transporting people as well as all kinds of goods in both directions. Voices shouted to one another across the water and the sounds of horses and carts moving along the streets provided a constant backdrop to the setting.

Many of the workmen were deep chocolate in colour, reminding everyone that this was indeed Africa, where dark-skinned people were the original inhabitants. The business citizens were primarily Dutch or English, with some Malays. Slavery was unfortunately still a way of life, especially on the farms, although a law to abolish slavery was apparently imminent, according to Captain Fielding. The city had suffered from repeated wars between the Dutch and the British over the years, resulting in the latest victory by the British last year, 1809.

The Captain, officers, carpenter and cooks went ashore to find supplies and items for small repairs to the boat. It took a couple of hours for everyone to find their 'land-legs' again, but they all enjoyed their explorations. The Captain checked in with the authorities, giving details of his prisoner contingent. He recorded the death of the baby and indicated he had one sailor for local confinement and trial. He handed over his notes summarizing the crime, with his and the militia commander's signature appended.

A number of ship chandleries and warehouses lined the harbor edge, and it didn't take long to find the replacement materials they needed. They were promised delivery the next morning early so as they could start the repair work quickly.

A great deal of time was spent in the local marketplace, where an amazing assortment of goods was on display, in particular pungent spices and wild animal meat and exotic animal skins, many of the latter being quite new to the English men. Some hides were made into crude coats or small vests, but most noteworthy were women's hats with ostrich plumes. Captain Fielding bought some ostrich feathers to take home to Mrs. Hutchinson. The biggest surprise was the range of native flowers and plants for sale. Table Mountain housed several mini-climates, and the visitors were told there were more indigenous plant species there than in the whole of the British Isles. The cooks bought meat, and vegetables, including corn, and a variety of fruits, but especially lemons and limes to bolster their citrus inventory and help the fight against scurvy.

Back on board the *Surrey,* in the absence of any ship motion, the guards were enjoying the sunshine and watching the prisoners lackadaisically since they were expecting no trouble. However, two of the convicts couldn't resist the opportunity and dove overboard and tried to swim to shore. The first was pulled from the water into one of the numerous boats plying the harbour, and while the other made landfall, he was quickly apprehended by the local constabulary and returned to the ship, where chains and irons denied them both further attempts at escape, or upper deck fresh air.

The minimal repairs were effected quickly and after two days at rest the ship was nearly ready to depart. The Captain penned another letter to his housekeeper.

Dear Mrs. H.,

We are experiencing beautiful sunshine in Cape Town, and the crew and prisoners are relaxed after a heavy crossing of the Southern Atlantic. It is an interesting town with a mix of people working here – from dark skinned Malay and African natives to Dutch and English running the various businesses. As usual, ships' chandlers with their warehouses occupy the streets surrounding the main jetty, and you'd be surprised at the preponderance of proprietors' names with Dutch heritage such as Stellenbosch, Paarl, Tulbagh, Plettenberg, Uitenhage, and Graaff-Reinet. There is a giant Commercial Exchange building which seems out of proportion to others, but represents the influence that merchants and traders have in the Colony.

The marketplace is huge and offers many varieties of meats, fruits, and vegetables that we have never seen before, along with the hides of exotic animals. It seems strange to see well-dressed ladies with servants carrying parasols shopping at the pathetic little stalls. I have a surprise for you that I acquired there, but you'll have to wait for it, I'm afraid.

We learned that there are more plants and flowers grown here than back home. That was definitely a surprise, given how important gardening is to us Brits. We were also lucky enough to be given a tour of a typical house, where everyone was impressed with its extremely high wooden beamed ceilings and airy room arrangements. Much different to jolly old London!

The trip has had its usual ups and downs. Unfortunately, a baby boy born in the terrible equatorial heat succumbed just two days after birth. It was terribly sad for the mother and affected many of us. A massive storm shortly afterwards had us going backwards on our direction, but we gradually regained our position and moved on, picking up strong westerly winds 30 degrees south of the equator. They propelled us quickly to Africa.

An ugly incident occurred when one of the sailors beat up one of the female prisoners very badly. He's now with the civil authorities here, and the girl is recovering slowly. I try to be friendly and reassuring to all the convicts, but it seems you can't please everyone, even though they are much better off than those on other convict ships. Two men tried to swim ashore here, but they are now in the ship prison. I was hoping not to have bad prisoners but clearly that was a misguided expectation. (Most of them are well behaved though).

From what I have learned both before leaving, and here in port, the trip across the southern Indian Ocean will be very cold. If we are lucky, maybe we will see some of the whales that reside there. I will be offering the women prisoners the woolen supplies to use for whatever purposes they deem appropriate. I wish you could see how well they have done with the lightweight cottons. I'm sure they will do as well with the woolens. I can only commend you on your purchases. Many of the women owe their comfort to your purchases. Thank you, my dear.

I imagine the leaves on the trees in the parks are starting to turn color about now. I hope you are getting some exercise and not staying inside all day. Make sure you keep warm when winter comes by keeping the fire alight.

I need you to stay healthy and well.

Your devoted friend.

Captain Fielding

With everyone, except prisoners in the onboard gaol, feeling refreshed, the *Surrey* pulled out of port. Hundreds of citizens lined the shores, watching the impressive boat leave their harbour. North and west out of the harbour then turning sou'southwest after Mouille Point, the ship ran gently down the coastline before turning true south, and eventually southeast, to round Cape Point by nightfall.

The Indian and Atlantic oceans collide somewhere south of a line between Cape Pont, twenty-five miles south of Cape Town, and Cape Agulhas, one hundred miles as the seagull flies, to the southeast of Cape Town. Coming straight from Antarctica, the cold Benguela Current flows northwards up the west coast of Africa, while around the east and south coasts the warm Mozambique Current flows from the equator and almost doubles back on itself when it meets the

Benguela Current. Wrecks have littered the coastline since the fourteen hundreds, when Portuguese sailors first attempted the passage. The meeting of the two currents causes the waves to hit one another at oblique angles and then join to form a single, larger wave. Coupled with fierce winds circulating from the west, it is an area that all mariners accord the greatest respect.

Every crew hand was on deck as the *Surrey* veered well south of the coastline with the wind behind her. The sails were full hoping to catch the maximum breeze in order to generate as many knots as possible. The main concern was the potential frequency and size of the waves ahead. The hatches and ventilation shafts were battened down and the prisoners were told to find something sturdy to hang on to. A rough ride over the next ten hours or so was fully expected.

The boat was tossed around like a cork, the strong westerly providing the main force helping the boat retain stability and direction. Two huge waves came on nearly broadside in the first fifty miles, heeling the boat well to starboard and scaring even the most experienced sailors. The shouts and screams from below exacerbated their nervousness. Through it all Captain Fielding stood resolutely firm behind the helmsman, radiating a sense of confidence that was an inspiration to those watching. Land could be seen to port for a while, but gradually it receded into the distance as the coastline angled northeast. Night fell, and the sailors were thankful that the moon was three quarters full and there were limited clouds. None of the crew was permitted to sleep. All eyes were needed to watch the waters ahead. The cooks kept up a supply of hot soups and bread, but no spirits were allowed. Throughout the watch the Captain stood calmly.

As the sun broke through, tensions eased, for the sea was running calmer, and they were being propelled by both the wind and the Mozambique Current. The hatches were opened and the convicts allowed on deck in groups, although many stayed below and slept, having been awake for far more hours than usual.

For the next week only slow, awkward progress was made, with currents and gale-force storms throwing them ninety miles further south than desired. The more south they were pushed, the colder the weather. Even though it was spring in the southern hemisphere, someone had forgotten to tell Antarctica.

The Captain broke out the case of his special wine and shared it with his officers at dinner, hoping to inject some warmth and comradeship. It was a feeble attempt, he knew, for the weather was dreadful. Definitely not a good time, and destined to get worse. Icy rain pellets were driving at them under swirling winds from port, forcing any man on deck to turn his head away else get smitten with highly annoying stings on his cheeks and forehead. Even the protective rain gear didn't help much.

What the Captain anticipated was that soon, more than likely, the water would freeze on the rigging, masts, rails and cabins, and gradually build up into thick sheets of ice. The only solution would be for the able-bodied seamen to hack away with axes, breaking up the frozen clumps and tossing them overboard. The more ice that formed, the heavier the ship would become and the increased weight would slow down any progress they hoped to achieve.

There was another pending danger worse to deal with, however as they continued to be pushed south. Icebergs! The lookouts forward and to starboard had been doubled and were relieved every 60 minutes in the hope of keeping eyes fresh and alert. Hitting an iceberg in these waters would be disastrous. With the driving rain it was getting harder and harder to see ahead through the mist.

Just as the rain started to decrease in intensity, a small iceberg was sighted less than a quarter of a mile ahead off the port bow. This was a truly undesirable sighting which indicated they were already in the middle of an iceberg field, as they had expected the only icebergs to be off their starboard side, where the winds and rain had been driving them. Thankfully, the rain suddenly stopped, and through a break in the clouds a thin wedge of moon shone. It danced in and out of sight for the next two hours, but helped enormously as its wan light reflected off icebergs nearby.

As if God had decided to come to their rescue, the wind shifted to come from the west and the Captain immediately tacked northeast. Out of consideration for the prisoners he ordered the hatches unsealed to let fresh cold air into the hold. The first noise arising from below was the cry of a newborn, prompting the Surgeon to hurry down to check out the new baby. Mother was a little bruised from sliding around during the delivery process, despite the efforts of friends to hold her in place, but she was smiling as she held her little girl tightly and the Surgeon checked them both.

Out of the throes of misery in a terrible storm a small miracle had occurred. To have come through so well during a truly ugly sailing experience was a testament to many of belief in a higher authority.

Despite the cool temperature it was easier to keep this baby warm than it had been to keep the previous arrival cool, and as the ship worked its way northeast both the baby and mother thrived. Everyone took the baby's arrival as a good omen.

The Captain announced that finally they were sailing in the shadow of the south coast of Australia. Although this was where their penal colony home was to be found, the prisoners seemed relieved. The voyage had been much tougher on them than any had expected, and the anticipation of stability outweighed their fear of the unknown.

The predictions of the Surgeons in London in regard to marriages on board started to come true. In fact, it was Dr. Browning who first came forward with Ruth Wickham asking the Captain to marry them. The Surgeon was so taken with his bride-to-be that he was willing to live in Australia with her rather than journey back home. He figured he would easily be able to make a living as a doctor in the new land. When the news of the pending ceremony spread throughout the ship, three more couples came forward. Two pairs came from the prisoner ranks, and one female prisoner appeared with the second eldest guard, who also seemed sincere in giving up his opportunities back in England.

And so late on a clear breezy morning Captain Fielding used his Naval Command authority to declare the four couples formally married as man and wife, and recorded their new designations in the logbook against their individual names. The cooks, who proudly produced small cakes for each of the couples, as well as another 30 for the crew and prisoners to share, were showered with praise for having the creativity to produce so much from the dwindling stores. The sailors got an extra ration of rum, and on their request to the Captain, prisoners who wanted a drink were also offered a small quaff of the burning liquid.

Those who knew the English version of the newly emerging song from France, "For he's a jolly good fellow" sang it with gusto, teaching others who ended up joining in as the simple melody caught on.   It was one of those days when it felt good to be alive.

The weather slowly warmed and the wind propelled them forward. Just as the lookout called "Land ho" as he sighted the coastline off the port bow, those at the starboard rail saw two giant whales send their spume skyward.   It was yet another great day and the coincidence of the two sightings was remarked upon for days afterwards. The coastline grew closer and then one day there was an island dead ahead, signaling their entry into Bass Strait north of Van Diemen's Land.

Two more couples from amongst the prisoners came forward seeking the Captain's blessing in marriage, to which he happily agreed. Strangers committing to marry after a maximum of two months getting to know one another? Seemed like a short courtship in his view and he wondered how long such 'marriages of convenience' would last. On the other hand perhaps the newness of the unknown would help the bonding experience as they faced unpredictable challenges together. He'd probably never know. One of the men was George Farnborough, who was holding hands with Anne Mooney, who had turned out to be a wonderful teacher, loved by boys and girls alike. Obviously George had overcome his lack of faith in humanity, and had picked up interaction habits that had been rewarded. Anne had found a strong, handsome mate with a valuable profession that would undoubtedly be in demand. She had made a wonderful transition from her old life.

North of Hogan Island a massive storm blew in from the southern boundaries of The Ditch, the stretch of water between Australia and New Zealand. It was a cruel blow so close to the end of the journey and was poorly received by both crew and passengers. It slowed down progress along the coastline of New South Wales, and when it finally cleared, the humidity was intensely cloying. As the Captain steered closer to shore, fires were sometimes spotted on sandy beaches. It made many on board nervous as they recalled talk of savages inhabiting the new land that they had heard before they left England.

Their fear was justified, as conflicts with the natives were weekly affairs at the edges of the towns. Unlike the friendly natives of Tahiti that Captain Cook had described and which had coloured expectations of government officials, these indigenous peoples with their more primitive nomadic culture did not appreciate the invasion of foreigners with their disrespect for the country they owned and loved.

But it was a day of high emotions when Captain Fielding finally turned the *Surrey* to the west and steered through the North and South Heads that marked the entrance to the waters of Sydney. As the ship was released from the ocean waves into calmer waters she fired two cannon to announce her arrival. A hush fell over the decks as everyone took in wondrous sights for sea-tired eyes. Rugged cliffs fell to rocky shores or sandy beaches, and heavily leaved trees in bright spring foliage rustled gently in the breeze. Small rivulets ran into the bay and a giant opening at one point showed another large bay to the north. Smoke curled skyward way ahead where the town laid in waiting. A family of natives pulled their nowie boats to shore and stood watching impassively, the children hiding behind their legs.

Two longboats appeared in the distance and steered toward the barque. A large rope net was dropped over the side and two men in guard uniform clambered aboard. One was a pilot designated to guide Captain Fielding to a pre-chosen anchor spot, the other an immigration official who stood by, waiting for the ship to come to rest. Into view came the tents and small wooden buildings marking the shores of Sydney town. Crowds of both whites and blacks lined the shores, the whites waving and cheering. And even though the prisoners knew this was a penal colony waiting for them, in a strange way they felt as if they were being welcomed, and waved back.

Little did they realize that the Europeans were cheering in anticipation of a flood of new supplies of food, animals, and industrial and agricultural implements. More prisoners unfortunately meant more crowding in existing housing and more mouths to feed from government stores. Cargo ships received more attention than convict ships, but they were few and far between, as the Colony was only a little over 20 years old. By any standards it was still an undeveloped, untamed land, and the authorities were still experiencing unexpected challenges due to the country's primitive conditions and little-understood native inhabitants.

But to those on board, compared to the months at sea with unchanging landscapes and at the mercy of violent storms, this was civilization on terra firma, where the threat of being shipwrecked and drowning in monstrous seas was no longer relevant. The anchors were set bow and aft, and two more cannon were fired as a tribute to their safe arrival. The first stage of their new life was complete.

No individual on board really knew what the next stage held in store. Some would welcome it, some would hate it. And the latter would outnumber the former by a large margin.

Welcome to the penal colony known as Botany Bay.

Part Three – New South Wales

Chapter 20

Officials from the second longboat crowded into the Captain's cabin.   The representative from Customs was interested in the supplies. Another official left to talk to the Militia Commander, while the remaining two sought summary information from the Captain and the Surgeon about the voyage itself, and the numbers and conditions of the prisoners and crew.   They were amazed to find only one infant death along the way, and only one sailor left behind in Cape Town.

Since it was late afternoon they agreed that the muster and disembarkation process would start early the next morning. First off would be the married couples, followed by single women with children, then single women traveling alone, and finally the single men. Crew would be last off after the Militia had left.   It would take two days to complete the process, as there were only a few longboats available to carry passengers ashore along with their scant belongings which had been held in escrow by the Militia in closed quarters.

The Captain announced the plan to those on board and asked the cooks to prepare a special feast to celebrate their final meal, or penultimate meal for the men, together.   He offered up the remaining cases of the personal red wine he held and ordered one of the pigs and several ducks slaughtered for the occasion. The cheers were easily heard across the waters and the officials rowing back to shore turned in surprise wondering what the enthusiasm was about on the newly arrived ship now gracing the waters of Sydney Cove.

In the middle of the night a faint tapping on the door announced young Margaret Ebbit's arrival to the Captain's cabin. She stayed till first light, giving him a new range of memories of sexual satisfaction. It was her only known way to say thanks. She had been in the class of adult students taught by Sarah Killeen and was now able to write, based on Sarah's intensive tutelage. Her minister father had taught her to read from the Bible early in life, but teaching writing had been reserved for her elder brother. She knew her sexual appetite would probably get her into trouble one day, but for the moment it was something she could not quell. Captain Fielding wished her well, wherever her life might lead, and promised to put in a good word for her when the authorities asked.

Before the couples departed for shore next morning a large crowd gathered around the Captain and Margaret proudly presented him with a gift and a letter signed by all the prisoners who could write. She read the letter out loud so those who could not read could understand what was in it.

LETTER TO CAPTAIN FIELDING

Sydney, October, 1810

> DEAR SIR — We, the undersigned prisoners per the ship *Surrey*, on her late voyage from Gravesend in England, to this port, beg, on our own part, as well as on that of all the other prisoners by this vessel, to request your acceptance of the accompanying carving of an albatross, which bird we honor as a symbol of friendliness, as our joint testimonial of esteem and respect towards you, as the commander of the vessel in which we made so long and victorious a voyage to this colony, from our native land. Your respect for the peoples of this ship

as humans first, prisoners second, has caused all to be thankful, as has the education you provided many, and the small blessing in clothes and board games and books you have bestowed upon us.

We thank you sincerely and wish you a prosperous voyage back to England. Hoping and trusting that the divine blessing may attend you in your future course, we are,

There followed over 150 signatures and a number of 'X's from those unable to write. The albatross had clearly been carved patiently by a master artisan, one of the prisoners. When the Captain asked who that was, an older gentleman stepped forward and shook hands. Sam Hitchins, from the fishing village of Looe, in Cornwall, had long carved herons and gulls from driftwood, earning welcome pennies from the limited number of tourists who passed by his shack. He showed the Captain where he had carved his name underneath the bird's tail.

For a few moments, the Captain was speechless, overwhelmed by the unexpected gratitude shown. He finally stood on a box and a hush fell across the crowd. They knew this might be the last occasion most of them would see or hear him, and that the future may not be as forgiving or as supportive as he had been. He looked from face to face, saw smiles and thankfulness, mixed with a sense of uncertainty that was entirely natural under the circumstances. His speech was short. "For a bunch of land-bound citizens, you have done incredibly well sailing for months across two of the world's most unforgiving oceans, and I salute your perseverance and fortitude. I also thank you for trusting in me and my crew to get you here safely. Your gift will long be treasured. I hope you will look upon this place as one of opportunity. For some I know that will be harder than for others. In any event, may the Lord bless you and hold you in his hands as you face the future. I wish you all well."

Tears formed at the corners of many eyes, and the Captain turned quickly and headed for his cabin, as the first sets of married couples were shepherded to the rails and down into the longboats. The Captain pulled his extra trunk out and noticed that its only remaining content was the beautiful chess set he had indulged in the first day he and his housekeeper had gone shopping. People had noticed it when other goods were unpacked but no one had shown interest in playing, so it remained unopened. Maybe someone amongst the government officials in town might like a game, he thought. Time would tell.

The Superintendent of Convicts sorted the women into two groups. Those with specific previously paid-occupations such as teachers, maids, cooks, governesses, nurses etc were in one relatively small group and were taken ashore first. When they were landed, the rest were loaded into larger boats to be taken directly 15 miles up-river to the Female Factory in Parramatta where they would be housed and employed in making garments for male prisoners working on the chain gangs.

It was a poignant time as friends were separated, not knowing what destiny awaited them and wondering if they'd ever see each other again. Children, not understanding, cried also, adding to the general atmosphere of misery and despair. The immigration people understood, as they'd seen it before, so their urgings to 'move along' were more tolerant than might otherwise have been the case. Many prisoners also felt a slight case of abandonment.   For over three months the *Surrey* had been their temporary, albeit mobile, home.   They'd become used to its behavior – the creaks, groans, leak spots, protruding floor boards, and low ceiling timbers, as well as how she rolled and bucked, and where the stairs were unstable, and how the hatches were opened and closed. What sort of roof would be over their heads this very night, they wondered, as they clambered down the rigging and their mattress and pillow were handed down behind them? No one had even hinted at what lay ahead, and just as surprisingly no one had asked. Their trust in Captain Fielding had implicitly been transferred to the authorities in Sydney.

A bigger mistake could not have been made.

The skilled women put ashore at the Quay were immediately parceled out to various tents and buildings where in most cases they found fellow inmates. They were told to assemble in the main square the following morning at 8 am sharp, when they would receive their assignments. A few might stay in town to help in a bakery or a start-up school, while others would be transported to a farm or other town or country abode where different skills were needed – perhaps as a governess or a cook. A complicated system of requests and referrals dictated the appointment of individuals to specific positions. The individuals per se had no input and had to follow the instructions handed out, or be branded as trouble makers and immediately sent to prison in Parramatta. Individuals were not treated as humans but pieces of government chattel processed to meet impersonal requests on paper.

The following morning the men began moving ashore. Even though there were more of them than women, the process was much faster as there were no children to manage and the men could carry their loads more easily. By 1 pm they were all assembled at the park-like space at the end of the jetty. They were then marched through the town to a large open space where they were arranged in two lines for the inspection of Governor Macquarie. The Governor's party consisted of Captain Fielding, Dr. Browning, the local Superintendent of Convicts, and the Chief Engineer. Based on citizens' requests signified to the magistrates of the different regional districts, along with the needs of the Chief Engineer, assignments had been prepared the previous evening using information from the notes made by the Captain and Surgeon during the voyage.

The Superintendent proclaimed the specific prisoner's destination and the Governor asked for comments from the Captain and Surgeon on the behavior of the individual, sometimes suggesting alternative destinations but usually agreeing with what had been decided in advance. When finished, he addressed the group, asking whether anyone had a complaint to make arising from treatment on the voyage or otherwise. Any complaint registered would have been passed to the police to investigate later. As expected, there were none raised against Captain Fielding. The Governor then gave a formal address, expressing his hope that the change which had been effected in each convict's situation would lead to a change in their conduct and that they would become new men. Most of the convicts understood that these were simply 'official words' that had to be delivered by rule but which had no real sincerity behind them.

The Governor's next words, however, were a surprise. "While you are a prisoner in this Colony, you should be aware that no reference will be made to the crime in your past. It is how you behave in the future in your respective assignments that will alone entitle you to reward or indulgence. Please remember that. Welcome to Australia."

Turning to the Captain and Surgeon, he said "Gentlemen, it would be my pleasure to have you dine with me this evening. Doctor Browning, please bring your lovely wife. Thank you for your help today, gentlemen. I look forward to chatting further with you later."

Chapter 21

Climbing back on board after dinner with the Governor, the Captain was surprised at the lack of noise. There was laughter from the crew's mess room as the last drunk stragglers closed out the night, but no one was on deck; the militia had departed along with the prisoners. And Dr. Browning had stayed ashore with his wife at the Governor's house. Perhaps it wasn't the lack of noise as much as loneliness that he felt. Tomorrow he would give most of the crew several days off while he oversaw the Government Stores laborers unloading the goods he'd brought on the ship as cargo. His list of supplies had brought smiles all round due to both its quantity and variety. Instead of grumbling, he had heard snippets of praise for what the naval officials back in England had put together, goods far more useful than those other ships had apparently brought. It occurred to him that this whole business of setting up not just a penal colony, but a civilization, in a new country was a learning experience at both ends.

In certain ways like the voyage itself that he'd undertaken. He'd tried new arrangements with the prisoners that were markedly different from the suggested naval rules for transport, and had been successful with them. He realized he'd have to be judicious in how he expressed his findings, which would be widely read back at Admiralty House.

Dreams that night were different than before. A baby boy tore the hat from his head, and a giant sperm whale smashed the stern of his vessel. The mizzen mast cracked and was held in place by two albatrosses. A nude woman scratched his back in anger and strips of skin fell on the sheets. He finally woke, dreaming that he was gagging on fiery spirits smuggled on board at Cape Town. The bedcovers were on the floor and the remaining sheet was a wrinkled mess. He was sweating profusely.

Disturbed at the lingering memories of his dream, he dressed and headed for the prisoners' quarters with a lamp, seeking a positive reminder to quell his disquiet. The space between decks was eerily empty and silent. A child's yellow hair ribbon had caught where two spars joined. He pulled it loose and pocketed it. He passed by the small 'conjugal' room, noting that the dividing sheets were gone, although the ropes still hung across the upper beams. In the men's area a shadow crossing the floor signaled the presence of a rat. He swung the lantern to see where it went but it had disappeared without a trace.

Given his large bulk he found himself bent over most of the time. But at one point between upper deck joists he was able to stand upright. Holding the lamp up high he found a Bible wedged into a cornice, no doubt forgotten by one of the taller convicts. He retrieved it and tucked it inside his jacket. He felt encouraged to know that it had been revered, but at the same time felt sorry that it had been left behind. There was no sign of any of the games he had distributed, but he was glad to learn that they still were treasured. Eating utensils were piled tidily in places. Buckets were stacked inside one another. It looked like there had been a sense of pride within the quarters. Remnants of the wrongs in his dream washed away as he sensed the communal atmosphere that had taken place among the men. Silently, he once again wished them all well.

He went down another level into the cargo hold. There was hardly any room to move, and he knew it would be a difficult job come morning to get everything out unscathed, especially the large pieces of equipment. He was glad that wasn't his job. He retreated quickly, realizing he would see the total volume of merchandise tomorrow. No need to go examining its condition now.

Back on deck he looked to the north shore and spotted several fires. No doubt aborigines keeping snakes at bay. He wondered what exactly the natives thought about these strangers who arrived by water in their unusual winged floating machines. What did they think when they heard the cannons fire? Thunder not made in the sky? What did they think of the coverings the visitors wore over their skin? Were they different underneath somehow? Embarrassed not to show what nature had provided when they were born? And why did they cut down trees and make huts from the wood when great sheets of bark were available to make shelters?

The one thing that the present Europeans did have in common with the natives was the ability to catch and eat fish from the big waters. But was that all? He would obviously learn more the longer he stayed.

It took the whole day to unload the provisions in the holds deep below the water surface. The copper sheathing and extra insulation had done a remarkable job, as had the bilge pumps by never failing. Water under the pallets was minimal although the effects of the damp and humidity would surely show once the food bags and barrels were opened and inspected ashore. The main food supplies included flour, sugar, and salt, with barrels of salted pork, probably of dubious condition by now. Vast quantities of seed such as corn, wheat, and oats and a major contingent of rum barrels filled the forward part of the hold and were extracted first. Tons of agricultural and industrial tools, from screwdrivers to log splitters, ball bearings to ploughs, engraving tools to giant two man saws, and cauldrons, ropes, chains, blacksmith irons, huge bellows and an amazing variety of other useful items were retrieved from the middle of the hold. The final pieces unloaded were consignments of furniture and personal items that officials and free settlers had ordered, including ornate garden statues and European building materials such as marble slabs for houses of the landed gentry.

Once the supplies were removed the ship rode higher in the water. All the hatches and scuttles were opened in an attempt to increase airflow throughout the ship and remove the stale smells of the holds. The Captain and remaining crew hoped for rain to help wash the ship down, but none was immediately forthcoming. While some of the crew toured the town or visited Parramatta, the remainder helped check for any necessary repairs. The sails were taken down and inspected, the animal pens were cleaned, the rigging was greased, the cannon balls re-stacked and the huge cooking pots scrubbed till they shone. Mattresses were brought on deck and aired, uniforms and underclothes were washed and hung to dry.

Captain Fielding and the carpenter toured the local chandlers looking for the necessary items and workmen to make repairs. Nothing major was needed; rather a lot of little things. One spar needed strengthening, several rope block and tackle components needed replacement, and pitch for caulking small cracks in the upper hull. A few hemp sails needed patchwork repair, but generally speaking, the ship had held up well. It was new after all.

The Captain's focus now switched to finding cargo for the return trip, along with crew and potential passengers. There was an implicit assumption that most of his previous crew would return with him, but several of the more adventurous had already indicated their interest in staying behind. Passengers would actually impose extra costs, as cabins would have to be built to accommodate them. That took time and money and the Captain was reluctant to prolong his stay as far as he could see at the moment. There was nothing to attract him to this place. Maybe in years to come his opinion might change. At the moment it looked like a foreign outpost of a very primitive nature.

A local official offered to introduce the Captain to warehouse owners and brokers who would most likely be interested in sending exports back to Britain. The warehouse area was a motley collection of buildings around the secondary Darling Harbour, many still under construction. The lone wharf was being expanded, as trade in both directions was starting to pick up. The government deployed chain gang labor to build the wharf infrastructure, but private entrepreneurs paid to build the warehouses that were the critical aspect of their business.

The first broker visited had an unusual consignment of Wardian cases of native botanical selections which had been sent up from Launceston in Van Diemen's Land and were destined for the Royal Botanical Gardens back at Kew. These cases had glass fronts to observe growing progress so needed special packing.   Not the most valuable cargo, but Captain Fielding added it to his manifest. The flora and fauna of this Antipodean land were of major interest to botanists and naturalists back home. In discovering the country in 1770 Captain Cook and Joseph Banks had remarked on the unusual native plants and animals they observed. That which Banks brought back only served to fuel the curiosity for more information and discovery. The message had reached the outpost, and both live and dead animals and birds were collected for export. The unique fresh water platypus commanded the Captain's attention with its furry body, clawed legs, and duck's bill. As well, there were numerous examples of brightly colored lorikeets, and large cockatoos, some white with yellow crests, others black with powerful beaks. Preserved dingo, kangaroo, and koala hides were in piles ready for export. As much as he was intrigued, the Captain felt no desire to see any of the animals alive in their natural surroundings. He was definitely a sea man. For the live animals going back he would have to bring along a biologist.

There were two main commodities he was looking for to fill his ship's holds. They were seal skins and wool. Sheep growers had found that the Merino strain from Spain was a breed that produced beautiful fine wool on Australian grass. Even in the short period in which it had been cultivated so far, the wool was attracting major attention back in England. Weavers were starting to recognize that it was finer than European wool and they yearned for more product to test its consistency and reliability. The Captain asked Mr. Dalgety, the owner of one of the enterprises, about the sources of the bales he had stacked in his warehouse.

"Most of these have come from the north of Van Diemen's Land. The flocks there are relatively small yet, but we understand that the grass is lush around Launceston and there is plenty of water in the local rivers so it stays lush for most of the year. You see the bales at the back left of the store? Those come from out past Parramatta, and south near Camden. Brought in by bullock teams. The fleeces from Camden are outstanding, again because the land is more variable and with more trees and streams than near Parramatta where it is flatter and drier. Some of the natives tell us the land west of the Blue Mountains is also lush, but until someone finds a viable route across those giant hills we won't know for sure. I'm an optimist, Captain, and hoping wool becomes a major export of this land."

"Good for you, Sir. I hope you are right. How many bales are we talking about to take back to England for you?"

Mr. Dalgety called to his foreman. "Hey Hutch, what's our count today?"

"114 bales, boss," came the reply. "We're getting more every week."

"There you are, Captain. When do you plan to leave? I'll obviously have more if you've got two more weeks here."

"That's close to my target, Mr. Dalgety. I want to be eastbound before it gets too hot. I'll be happy to take 140 to

150 bales in 25 days. I presume you can have the appropriate official paperwork organized by then?"

"It's a deal, Captain. I'll guarantee you 150 bales in 25 days. Who is your agent here? Goldsborough, I presume?"

"Indeed. I'll send my representative by later this afternoon. By the way, I'm intrigued; are your warehousemen convicts or ex-convicts? I assume you and the other merchants are Free Settlers, but the workers are convicts or emancipists?"

"You got it, although there is one emancipist among us commercial owners who had money and has a smart business head, but he's just one out of the bunch. The good thing is that if a convict behaves well, depending on his sentence, he can be free in seven or even fewer years, and if he has skills from back home there's nothing to stop him setting up some form of enterprise here. Without those folk this place would be a lot worse off, believe me. And frankly I'm not sure about the justice system back home. Many of the convicts are decent people underneath, who stole something trivial to pawn in order to buy food. I think the punishment handed out in many cases was totally out of proportion to the crime.

"Take Hutch there. Came out in 1803. Got his Absolute Pardon last month. Got his Ticket of Leave four years ago on my recommendation. I feel real proud of his commitment. Can't do without him, although he talks about going home every now and then. Don't know why he doesn't find a nice woman and settle down.

"Now, Blue, the red-haired chap with him over there, is one of the convicts currently assigned to me, like Hutch initially. I have three who help load and unload, haul the heavy stuff around. Couple could be troublemakers, but it helps that Hutch has been in their shoes. Usually can quieten them down. Wouldn't be surprised if one of them asks you about a ride home. Don't encourage them. None of the others have their Pardons yet."

"You obviously care for this Hutch fellow. Tell me what more you know about him. I'm intrigued. Where does he come from? And what was his crime? How did he get assigned to you?"

"One of the good things here is that the government officials are really trying to build up the commercial side of the town so it isn't just a penal colony. And with the emerging richness of resources turning up around the countryside it looks like there'll be good opportunities for trade. Each year I ask for one more strong man from the arriving convict ranks. I don't care what they've done in a previous life or what their crime was, I need brawn and a few smarts to move the heavy bales of wool around. Ordinarily, with no real trade skills, the men I get would end up on a chain gang, but the officials think I'm a good boss, and assign me someone who can help with the business growth. Some of the chaps I get can be a bit rough and I've had to let two go in past years, which is why Hutch is such a great addition.

"What do I know about him? Very little. Comes from Devon somewhere, worked in the tin mines, was caught selling mine property pick-axes, got seven years as a result. Seems to have an attitude to make up for bad things in his past. Works hard. Strong as an ox."

"Mr. Dalgety, wait a minute; I have a hunch I know this fellow. I come from Portsmouth, but know of a Hutchinson family from Plymouth. Presumably his full name is Hutchinson?"

"That's correct, but we've been calling him Hutch for years. It's a local Australian thing to shorten people's names – think the sun makes us lazy down here or something."

"What's his Christian name?"

"I knew you were going to ask that. It's Ed for Edward, but only when he's mad at himself do I ever hear him use it. Otherwise he's simply Hutch.

"Speaking of names, please call me Fred. We're far less formal here than back home."

"Amazing. Maybe I can catch up with him later. Must get more business out of the way first. So, tell me Fred, who is the best merchant at handling seal skins and seal and whale oil? I want to fill the ship with as many skins as possible."

"Well now, that's a conundrum, Captain. Down the dock walk a bit there's a chap named Simon Long. He's clearly an entrepreneur, dabbling in lots of different enterprises. He actually prefers to ship goods in his own vessels. Your timing may be propitious, however. He recently bought a boat but the Captain he hired absconded with it in Fiji and so he has no transport at the moment. He's a big sealer, financing his own expeditions. Ordinarily he would transport his own goods, but if he has a lot of skins and oil stored he may be anxious to ship them off rather than waiting for months to buy another ship. I know him a little. Happy to walk along and introduce you if he's present!"

"Aye, that would be grand, Fred. I appreciate the offer. May I buy you lunch somewhere first?"

That afternoon the Captain found Mr. Long to be very cagey about any interest in having his seal hides and whale and seal oil shipped to England on the *Surrey*. It was clear that he was in a bind with thousands of skins and hundreds of barrels of oil in his warehouse. He kept hinting that he'd probably have his own ship available soon and would prefer to wait for that, but in case the arrangements didn't work out, he'd like to stay in contact over the next two weeks and check with the Captain before he set a date for departure.

One of the disconcerting things about the new country was the awkwardness and inadequacy of international communication. It took at least ten months, more likely a year, to manage turn-around communication with England, as boats often took 5 months to travel one way, assuming they even made it. Communication with Van Diemen's Land was better, although far from perfect.

There'd been information from the last ship that had arrived from Hobart that another ship was in dock there loading independently owned seal products which had recently arrived from the islands in the south of New Zealand. But there was no information on when it was likely to leave and head for Sydney. Nor how long it might take, as there were no advance weather forecasts. Three days, seven days? It depended on whether there were storms or contrary winds along the way.

The Captain set his strategy for negotiation. He would not contact Mr. Long again unless the Hobart freighter did not turn up during the next two weeks. He talked to the Sydney agents for the ship who promised him first rights of onward carriage, and waited hopefully. Seal products were more valuable than wool at the time. The skins were primarily taken to either England or China and sold for use as material for hats, coats, waistcoats and boots. Seal and whale oil was finding increased demand for lighting, lubrication and manufacturing, as the industrial age came more and more into prominence. There was no demand for seal or wool products in Australia, although entrepreneurs, including Simon Long, were thinking about establishing textile mills.

Repairs on the *Surrey* were completed, three new crew members were recruited, and provisions for the return trip ordered. It now became a waiting game to see if the Hobart freighter would turn up before the ship's scheduled departure. On the twelfth day small cannon fire and a beacon lit on South Head announced its arrival. Captain Fielding had his ship towed to Darling Harbor, where the transfer of seal products was immediately undertaken.

It didn't take long for Simon Long to arrive on the scene. "Captain, I'd hate to see you going home half-full. So I'd be willing to send along a portion of my skins and oil at, let's say half the prevailing cargo rate, to make your trip more profitable. I'm sure your masters back home would appreciate it. I've heard that my ship is coming back from Fiji and should be here in two weeks', but I'm sure by then I'll have more supplies to fill its holds."

Taken aback by the man's arrogance, but revealing nothing, the Captain responded pleasantly, "That's very thoughtful of you, Mr. Long. I'll be happy to consider your proposition when I see how much wool is ready to travel."

In the pub at the end of the day the Captain conferred with Fred Dalgety and Hutch. The wool broker had nearly 160 bales ready for transport, and Hutch knew of 12 more promised in three days. Hutch leaned forward over the small table and said conspiratorially, "By the way, Captain. I know several of the chaps working for Mr. Long. I can tell you, he has no idea of when his boat will be back, if at all. He frets constantly about it so everyone who works there knows. And yes, one of his boats is due back from New Zealand with more seal products, supposedly in a few weeks, although the exact timing could be longer. However, he's short on storage space and will need to build more to accommodate it all if the load is anything like previous expeditions. So he desperately needs to move a lot of those goods currently in store. You could probably demand a small premium to take on some of his stock."

"Well, thank you, Hutch. That's very useful information. Very helpful.

"If you don't mind, I've been meaning to ask you something about your background. You have a familiar look about you, and based on what Fred has told me, I think I know why. Where exactly do you come from in Devon?"

"Plymouth was where I grew up, Captain. Why do you ask?"

"Were you born in 1784?"

"Indeed I was. I presume that's significant in some way?"

"This is going to come as a major shock, but I'm pretty sure you must be the long lost son of a lady I know well. Was your mother named Anne, and your father William?"

Hutch's eyes clouded over and his jaw dropped in amazement. "How on earth do you know that, Sir? Even Mr. Dalgety here doesn't know that much."

 "Because I'm a very fortunate man, that's why, Hutch. You see, your mother is my housekeeper back in London. She's been with me for years now. It's unbelievable to find you here."

Fred interrupted. "This is absolutely uncanny. How many Hutchinsons must there be in this country by now? A dozen maybe? More? How many about the same age as Hutch? Most probably, but let's say half at least. Probably a number of them also in Sydney hereabouts. Others up country. And yet by the longest of odds the one you meet here is someone you've known about but never met.

"Am I hearing that your mother doesn't know you were convicted and transported, Hutch? And so she's wondered all these years where you are? Poor woman. Why is that? And what about your father?"

"Maybe I can answer, Fred, to save Hutch a little embarrassment. He left home and went to the collieries because his father would come home drunk and beat his mother. Which happened far too often. His father died when he was drunk and cracked his head falling down on the docks where he worked. I imagine you did know that much, right, Hutch?"

"He was a totally rotten man, and I didn't learn about his death until two years after it happened. My mother would come to the mines wanting to see me. I was ashamed that I'd run away, left her on her own with father; I couldn't face her. I watched her leave one time, and she turned and saw me. I waved my cap, and even at a distance I could see that she recognized me. I decided then and there to find a way to give her money, for I knew Father had died. So I sold some of the excess property around the mine – lamps, pickaxes, rope, buckets, etc., but got caught. Kept the few shillings I'd made but was hustled off to gaol before I could give the money to her. My pleas for someone to tell her where I was fell on deaf ears, as I was just one of many able-bodied chaps about the same age. The gaolers only paid attention to the ten year old waifs who were locked up, trying to find a church or a parent to take them away from the lockup. And they convicted me and arranged my transfer to Middlesex gaol all in the space of a week. I guess they didn't want me in the Plymouth gaol. It happened so fast. Three weeks after I was convicted at the Assizes I was on a ship bound for Botany Bay.

"Please, do tell me about mother, Captain. Did she re-marry? Is she in good health? How did you come to know her?"

"It's a long story son. How about I tell you what I know over supper tonight? OK?"

Chapter 22

Simon Long came strolling along the dock where Hutch and his convict helpers were bringing wool bales out of store ready to be hoisted onto the *Surrey.* "Captain Fielding, I thought you'd be wanting some of my seal products to fill your holds, rather than the wool I see being prepared."

"Ah, then your judgment is way off, Mr. Long. I can make more with this cargo of wool than with your proposed cut rate fees for seal transport. I understand your offer, Sir, but I have no interest in it. Now, if you'll excuse me, I must see to the loading here." With that the Captain walked off to the Dalgety office.

Mr. Long strode after him. "Captain, perhaps I was a bit hasty in my earlier proposal. Suppose I pay 75% of your usual fees, instead of 50%. I'm sure that would be more remunerative for you than shipping wool."

Slowing his strides, stopping and turning, the Captain addressed the haughty man directly. "Let me make it quite clear, Mr. Long. Your pomposity is unacceptable, trying to take advantage of others in a humiliating fashion. I will take 100 barrels of oil and 10,000 skins at a carrying charge 15% above the normal fee. And I am being generous. I will negotiate no further. If you are interested you can let me know within the hour or I continue loading my wool. Bring your paperwork to Dalgety's office. I am leaving the day after tomorrow with or without your cargo. It makes no difference to me, but I'll not stand being judged as inferior to you simply because I am a sailor and not a merchant. Good-day, Sir."

Dismissed, shocked, and annoyed, Long strode off, harrumphing and muttering as he did so. Captain Fielding recounted his conversation to Fred and Hutch, adding, "Fred, you take double your usual commission out of the extra charges. Maybe share a portion of it with Hutch who gave me the impetus to stand up to him. I warrant he'll be back, but he'll deliberately make it two hours instead of one, in an attempt to reclaim some face. Irritating man.

"And Hutch. I guess that gives you a few more hours of breathing room to make your decision. Staying here or coming home with me? I hate to be thinking of stealing your best man, Fred. Up to him, really, although I must admit I'm trying to tempt him with passage as a working sailor. He'll have to prove himself to those in the crew already, but I doubt that will be an issue."

"And I'm truly torn, Captain. Boss, do you think you could manage without me for a year? Based on the Captain's information I would love to see my mother again, and I feel I owe it to her to take advantage of this incredible coincidence. I don't see that England has any attraction to keep me there. This country is where I belong now. I like it here, see boundless opportunity and no reason not to come back. Captain, will you be coming out again?"

"I'm sure I will, son. I'll guarantee you space coming back with me as a crew-man again.

"Fred, if I steal him away but promise to return him, older but wiser, will you still do business with me?"

Part Four – Homeward bound

Chapter 23

With only her topsails unfurled, the heavily laden *Surrey* pulled away slowly from the Darling Harbor dock, heading north then east around Dawes Point, past Sydney Cove, and along the Port Jackson stretch of water to the Heads. Once outside she slipped immediately into the heavy swells of the Tasman Sea. The rest of the sails were unfurled and a southeasterly course set for the southern tip of New Zealand, Land of the Long White Cloud.

Captain Fielding was pleased with his load. The cargo holds were filled almost to the point of overflowing, and he had received a handsome amount of fees for carriage, which he knew would make the Admirals very happy back home. He well recognized that his bonus would be drawn from the revenue. The more he brought home, the larger his stipend. His job now was to get there safely and expeditiously.

With no prisoners and no militia, this was going to be much more pleasant than the outward bound voyage. The *Surrey* rode a little lower in the water, but with the sails full he knew she still could make ten knots. Four new sailors, including Hutch, and a biologist happy to be going home. No surgeon. Perhaps it would be a little lonelier than the trip out, he thought.

The Sailing Master had the helm, so Captain Fielding stood at the stern, watching the last vestiges of the Australian coastline recede into the haze. The Tasman Sea could provide a rough crossing, he'd been told. Lying in the belt of westerly winds known as the "roaring forties," the sea was noted for its storminess. Stand easy now, the Captain told himself. No doubt you'll need to be strong in the days ahead.

He smiled at the thought of Hutch on board, and of his letter to Hutch's mother written soon after he'd arrived in Sydney a little over three weeks ago. A small cargo-only three masted schooner was scheduled to depart the town at that time and he'd written in haste before he'd even started looking for cargo brokers. He wondered what he would have written differently had he met Hutch before the schooner sailed.

Dear Mrs. Hutch,

We arrived in Port Jackson three days ago and are busy organizing the transfer of prisoners to the local authorities. It was a long, cold trip from Cape Town, but the crew and passengers survived it well. I have to share with you that the convicts gave me a beautiful wood carving of an albatross as a thank you gift for bringing them here safely. I know it is going to be a rude shock for many since the *Surrey* has been their home for 4 months and now they must find their land-legs. And face a totally uncertain future. Many will not fare well I am sure. Already I am surprised at how primitive conditions are here. Only a limited number of permanent buildings exist, no solid gaol; tents often house prisoners. Food is strictly rationed, so stealing from the commissariat happens frequently. There are unpleasant incidents with the natives, and law and order isn't operating as I would have expected. It's more like an open camp than a formal penal colony. I met the Governor who seems to have smart plans, but less control than he'd like. There are so many convicts here, outnumbering officials by ten to one, that they can make demands on hours they work that would never be acceded to back home. Yet I understand from a couple of the officials that up-country there is another settlement which is doing quite well, and that many of the early arriving convicts who have gotten their Tickets of Leave have set up small businesses such as bakeries and pubs, and brokerages moving locally grown produce down the Parramatta river to Sydney. Of course there is also major sea trade starting up in Sydney with the export of seal products and wool. I hope to bring some back as cargo on my return.

There are unusual and colorful animals – especially birds – and an amazing variety of fish to eat. Sydney Cove is actually quite beautiful, with sandy beaches interspersed between jutting cliffs and lots of trees down to the waterline. I'm told that the limited aborigines I've seen seem irritated and perplexed at the European presence. They are very dark, often wearing no clothing of any sort, but have ingenious little fishing boats, 'nowies', and long spears and 'throwing sticks'. They apparently have no permanent shelters but make temporary 'houses' called 'gunyahs' out of large sheets of bark off special trees, and eat animals they kill. They smell terribly.

There is a boat leaving tomorrow, so I'm sorry I can't tell you more about the place, as I haven't had time to really explore it as yet. I hope to be able to turn the ship around in about three weeks, so I imagine this letter will arrive about a month before I do if everything goes well. I promise I'll have much to tell you on return.

With the high heat of early summer here it's difficult to realize that soon snow will be falling back in London. Please be careful on the slippery streets and donate generously in my name to the carolers when they call at Christmastime. And as I write I realize this letter won't arrive probably until February, and Christmas will be behind you. Such is the timing of communication from the other side of the world.

With fond regards and warm friendship

Captain

Much had happened since writing his message and he'd learned a lot since. It would be fun sharing it once back in London.

It took seven days for the *Surrey* to get through multiple storms and reach the southwest corner of New Zealand's South Island. This was where the sealers and whalers came to the numerous islands and fjords, for their quarry abounded there. The scenery was magnificent with tall cliffs, waterfalls, and placid deep water in lengthy narrow bays that were eerily silent. At one of the fjords, curiosity and wonder made the Captain turn northward to explore, ever conscious that there was no chart for the sound he was in. Seals lay on the rocky shores of small islands in abundance, not even bothering to move as the *Surrey* swished past. Extra lookouts were in place watching for submerged rocks. All they encountered however were two large whales basking in the shallows. As they came up to the major waterfall at the head of the fjord and started their turn-around maneuver they heard a number of sharp cries.

Coming out from the rugged shoreline was a wooden long boat with ornate carvings on the sides and a massive decorated prow. Four men with tattooed faces were rowing with giant paddles and one was clearly calling out to the *Surrey*. Maoris! Native Polynesians from Tahiti and Fiji who'd settled the country a hundred years earlier. Europeans had limited experience of the natives, but had heard tales or their war-like fierceness and cannibalism. Tales from returning whalers and sealers were mixed, clearly reflecting the nature of different inland tribes.

The captain ordered sailors to the rail with muskets at the ready, but simultaneously had the rope nets lowered so the natives could climb aboard. The men, with seal-skin shawls draped across their chests and shoulders and wraps around their waists showed no fear, but as soon as they were on deck, squatted, removed their lower body coverings and laid them out on the deck. They then proceeded to place on them from hidden pouches in their shawls small fist-sized and larger stones and agates. It was hard to recognize the agates, for they were quite different from the ones the Captain had seen previously , which had brilliant colors and contours and needle spikes and varying shapes of crystals. These were of silver and gold hues, of odd shapes, not as dramatic in structure and formation as other agates, but attractive in their own way.

Other stones were markedly different, and Hutch identified them as nephrite jade from seeing them brought back to Sydney by sealers. Apparently the Maoris regarded well-formed stones that could be further carved into ornate shapes almost as treasures.   The sealers Hutch met had called the gems 'greenstone,' unable to pronounce the Maori word 'pounamu' without bringing gales of laughter from the traders.

Since this appeared to be a peaceful trade meeting Captain Fielding ordered the anchor to be dropped. The sailors saw the chance to take a unique gift home and wondered what the natives wanted in exchange.   They had axes, or at least adzes.   No one had indicated they wanted rum.   They had tools.   They had fishing lines.   Did they want mirrors and shiny beads like the natives of Tahiti that Captain Cook met? Certainly not wool and seal skins from the hold.   What then? Coal and lanterns and matches?   Maybe.   Animals?   The *Surrey* had a few pigs, lambs and hens on board for fresh meat supply.   Some of these were brought forward, but kindled no interest from the dark-skinned men.

Finally, one of the natives ceased talking, got up and walked along the rail stopping at one of the cannons and the pile of cannon balls, and gesticulating. Aha! They must have seen a cannon in operation at some stage and realized its potential value in a tribal war.   The Captain invited seamen with interest and funds to choose an agate or greenstone and place it on a large piece of canvas a sailor had set out. The Captain himself realized here was something unique he could take home to his housekeeper as a gift, and picked two of the finer pieces offered, one from each type of stone.

A group of sailors moved one of the cannons and the pile of cannon balls alongside the cloth, indicating this was their offer for the trade. The Maoris understood and after spirited conversation between them, two of their men went and retrieved another cannonball each from another pile and added it to their collection. A lot of head nodding sealed the deal.

Only one problem remained: how to get a heavy cannon to shore. But the Maoris were one step ahead. They'd noted how the cannon at the stern were much closer to the water. They'd also been far better prepared than the Captain and others had anticipated. With sharp cries directed to shore, two more boats suddenly came forth. They tied up alongside one another at the stern and put large planks across the three boats forming a carrying platform. A cannon there was disassembled, and three of their heftiest warriors picked it up, and with helpful support from their comrades climbed down and lowered it onto the planks. The individual cannon balls were handed from man to man and placed in the base of the boats.

Still not fully trusting the natives, the Captain launched two of his longboats which rowed to shore parallel to, but not too close to, the massive Maori boats. The weapon was reassembled and made stable on a rocky outcrop, and pointed at a small pinnacle of rock twenty yards away. The Quartermaster showed two of the natives how to prepare the powder and set the cannonball. He did this four times and then had them do it to his satisfaction. Finally he had the master gunner set the elevation for firing, and light the fuse. With a loud explosion the cannon ball smashed into the base of the pinnacled rock, causing hardly any damage. The gunner had done this on purpose to demonstrate the need for assessing the right angle of elevation. He now raised the barrel making sure the natives understood what he was doing. This time the pinnacle of rock was completely blown to smithereens, to the delight of the entire group. They got the message. Two men rushed off to retrieve the intact heavy cast iron balls.

The last act was to let the Maoris do everything on their own. They turned the cannon around and focused on a small grass and wood hut which had obviously been used as a shelter. One of the men clearly became in charge of the cannon and set it up ready to fire. He walked back and forth between the gun and the hut. Finally satisfied, a massive explosion sent the ball tearing through the thin walls bringing the whole shelter down. Once again a giant cheer like a war cry went up from the men.

The two English long boats pushed off, and returned to the *Surrey*, where the tales of what happened were appropriately embellished for those who'd stayed behind and only viewed things from afar. Knowing they'd have to reimburse the Admiralty for the loss of one cannon used for personal purposes, the trading group sat and argued about how to evaluate the worth of individual gems. They finally found an equitable solution that generated enough cash for a new weapon, and the Captain tucked the money away in the personal chest in his cabin.

They weighed anchor and moved quickly out of the sound to open water while the sun was still high in the sky. No other boats, English or Maori, were encountered as the barque made its way east to Foveaux Strait. Captain Cook had sighted the entrance to the strait during his circumnavigation of the south island in March 1770, but thought that Stewart

Island was joined to the mainland, so misjudged the Strait's nature. The openness of the Strait was not discovered until 1804, 6 short years ago. Joseph Foveaux was Lieutenant-Governor of New South Wales then.

Nine miles wide at its narrowest, thirty odd at its widest, and eighty miles long, it saved precious time getting through to the Pacific Ocean, although it required careful sailing with the heavy westerlies roaring from behind. Good practice for what lay ahead.

Hutch had gotten over his seasickness in the first 3 days, and with his superior strength quickly became the arm-wrestling champion on board. The same upper body strength also allowed him to move up through the rigging as fast as many of the more experienced hands, and as a result he was assigned to higher and higher cross spars and their sails. He and the Captain found one other area where they had coinciding interests – chess. On the ship that carried Edward to Australia, one of the crew had had a chess set. He befriended Edward and when time was available taught him how to play. This was the most thought-provoking activity young Hutch had ever engaged in, something totally new, and far different from the physical work he'd been involved in all his life. At first he found it very complicated but his teacher was patient, and after four months his pupil could think at least three moves ahead, which was an amazing effort for an uneducated lad.

Captain Fielding was rusty with his recollections, so that Hutch was able to win a few games as the Captain got back into more cerebral thinking. At the very least it filled the hours when the seas behaved and the wind was fair. Which happened about half the days they had needed to cross the southern Pacific Ocean in an east-southeast direction The wind and currents were generally behind them, but more frequently than expected, dark clouds would roll up from the south, bringing major rainstorms accompanied by thunder and lightning. When the seas built up as well, it was a roller-coaster ride of giant proportions, with 20 foot swells threatening to wash over them from behind. The well-built *Surrey* handled it all. Not perhaps with the utmost grace and agility, but with sturdiness and reliability.   Edward's preference was to work the forward mast in such conditions, being far more comfortable there than watching the waves at the stern from the aft mast.

The charts the Captain had of Tierra del Fuego, the Land of Fire, were very recent, and he was looking forward to the challenges imposed by the Magdalena Channel portion of the 350 mile long Strait of Magellan. This waterway separated the mainland portion of Chile from Tierra del Fuego, the set of imposing islands forming Cape Horn. In years past sailors had rounded the cape of South America through the bitterly cold and dangerous Drake Passage separating Cape Horn from Antarctica, notorious for turbulent and unpredictable weather, and frequented by icebergs and sea ice. Many ships didn't make it, and wrecks littered the rocky islands' shorelines. Even with these known conditions many sailing ships avoided the Channel due to the variable winds and currents and the narrow point along the way just over a mile wide with its treacherous currents.   Captain Fielding preferred the challenge of following winds, high tidal energy, and precision in course direction to facing highly volatile and unpredictable sea ice.

The *Surrey* arrived at the west coast of Chile north of its intended target, and ran south for two days before entering the Magdalena Channel. Most of the islands were unnamed, the narrowest margin being between the southern mainland and an island later named Isla Carlos III. Even that passage had exposed rocks and smaller islands in it, and Captain Fielding took the precaution of anchoring outside it and exploring the narrow passage by long boat before passing through. He waited a full day for a lull in the wind and favorable tides before safely traversing the gap. The reward for caution was the sighting of multiple pods of humpback whales at play.

At the southeastern end of the Channel the *Surrey* turned northeast into the wide portion of the Strait of Magellan. The Strait had been discovered in 1520 by Ferdinand Magellan, the Portuguese explorer and navigator in the service of Charles I of Spain. Small settlements of Spanish origin flanked the now-wide passage. The end ultimately was demarcated where it met the Atlantic Ocean by the four corners of Argentina and Chile.

Chapter 24

The voyage wasn't quite half-over yet, but to the crew it felt as if they had come through the worst, and now the way home was straightforward. Not really the case, as they paralleled the coast of Argentina, Uruguay, and Brazil, even turning to the northwest hundreds of miles east of Natal. Heavy southwest and southerly winds had them reaching the equator 5 weeks after leaving the Magellan Strait. Edward was appropriately introduced to King Neptune and his lengthy whiskers trimmed completely.

Maybe his mother would recognize him after all once they reached London in a month. He wondered what he would say to her. Captain Fielding suggested he wouldn't have to worry. His mother would have so many questions to ask that he would be too busy responding to have to take any initiative in that regard.

With short notice to decide whether to sail home with the Captain or not, Hutch had been rushed in making arrangements. He found a place to store his small set of belongings for a year, and left anything of sentimental or physical value with his boss, Fred, helping to ensure his return to the business. His biggest dilemma was choosing a gift for his mother. He wanted something meaningful that was uniquely Australian. The local birds were beautifully colorful and delightfully representative of the country, but impractical to bring back and be looked after. There were no natural gemstones available in Sydney, and the jewellery that was for sale had originated in Britain anyway.

He scoured the shops in George Street, Sydney, and raced to the Female Factory in Parramatta one day to see what the inmates had been knitting in their spare hours. The Warden was accommodating and after talking to several of the prisoners there, he struck a bargain with one woman who had made two beautiful long scarves out of the fine merino wool that passed through the establishment. Down by the river waiting for the packet ship back to Sydney he traded a bottle of rum for an ornate boomerang that a native was selling. And back among his favorite haunts by the Rocks, he found an old craftsman from whom he purchased a pair of soft ladies' gloves made out of supple kangaroo hide. The Captain assured him that his mother would be overwhelmed by his selections.

Beyond the equator they continued their northwest course until about latitude 30° north when they turned 90° northeast. Four days later as they picked up the westerlies, they veered a little more to the east, making England their direct target. With approximately two weeks to go Hutch approached the Captain with a question that had been roaming around his brain for a week or more. "How are we going to arrange for me to meet my mother? Should I find a place to rent in London and maybe come around one evening for dinner?"

"No, no, not at all, Hutch. When we arrive I shall have to spend two days at Admiralty House, basically providing summary details of my trips out and back. I'll be back there again a week later to go through the fine detail. It will take several days to unload our cargo and I'm going to ask you to help the officers check the condition of what is unloaded and keep accurate counts of the items as they are moved.

"When I'm at Admiralty House I'll send a note to your mother indicating I've returned and plan to be home late afternoon in two days' time after my de-briefing. I'll tell her that I'll be bringing along a young companion for few days and ask her to prepare the guest bedroom. You'll find it more of a closet than a true bedroom, I'm afraid, but bigger than what you've been sleeping in these past three months. I'll not say anything more about you. We've provided temporary lodging for others before so she won't think the request unusual.

"We'll work out the rest on the carriage ride home. Does that suit you?"

"it sounds very generous, Captain. I really am very thankful. And frankly, the closer we get to London the more nervous I become. I hope you have a drop of brandy at home. I suspect I will need it."

"More than a drop, lad. We may stop by a pub and buy a special bottle of wine for the occasion. Your mother and I often share a nice red wine from the continent.

"For now, forget about arrangements. I'll take care of them."

Just past Lizard Point, and after the celebrations at seeing English land again, a fierce storm slowed their progress, but they doggedly sailed on, finally entering the North Sea and making a successful run to the mouth of the Thames.

Home again!

Chapter 25

March 1811. The first signs of early Spring were helping restore smiles after a tough winter. It was still Napoleonic wartime, however. The Peninsular War was ongoing and in an unfortunate accident, Britain had recently lost a troop ship with 300 soldiers. In civil London, a major change had just been effected in the realm of royalty. George, the Prince of Wales, had become Prince Regent in February due to the perceived insanity of his father, King George III.

It was a strange historical and political period, with alliances that spanned the channel changing readily, an industrial revolution growing at home, trade across the world increasing, crime rising in major cities, and displaced returning soldiers being poorly repatriated by their government.

The first newspapers brought to the *Surrey* by the pilot ship out of Gravesend provided a disturbing update for the Captain and those able-bodied seamen who could read. Hutch's reaction was typical. "I think I may have been better off in Australia, thousands of miles beyond all this turmoil. How soon will you be headed back, Captain?"

Slowly but surely the pilot guided the huge ship up the Thames to the London Docks, Built only 12 years before, they were now a regular part of the London infrastructure. Housing Excise and Customs Departments, and with major warehouses strung out along the wharves, the docks were a hive of activity, employing hundreds of men in various capacities – from authoritative eye-shaded officials to burly wharfmen. The *Surrey* was carefully shepherded through the Shadwell Basin into the Eastern Dock and thence through Tobacco Dock into the larger Western Dock. With her valuable cargo she was given maximum attention and a prominent berth. At the time, these were the closest docks to the center of London, a huge government investment having been made in their construction. All major imports ended up here, and an eco-trading industry of massive proportions was born throughout the vicinity.

Hutch had never seen such an enormous collection of boats, many from foreign countries in unusual styles. Most of them were unloading luxury commodities such as ivory, spices, coffee and cocoa as well as wine. Barrels and cases littered the wharves, which were a hive of seemingly chaotic activity. Cargo rolled or was pushed down planks from the ships to the dock, then moved by porters in carts to the warehouses. Revenue men were everywhere, counting containers, casks and hogsheads, getting signatures on official forms, then escorting the buyer, owner, agent or Captain inside a long shed to finalize duties and taxes.

Handlers from nearby ships came strolling over especially to see the thousands of sealskins which were stacked in six-foot high piles, side by side, along the length of the ship. Dalgety's agent immediately brought extra men from his warehouse to help keep an eye on the prized cargo. The oil was already attracting buyers who had appeared out of nowhere once they heard it was available. The Captain smiled, knowing he'd done well taking on the extra oil he had stacked in the lower hold. Worth more than the wool on this particular trip.

After satisfying the customs and excise officials and conferring with the Dalgety's agent one last time, he gathered his ledgers and headed for the Naval office next to the big administration building. He quickly went through the roster of officers and able bodied seamen with the officials, indicating their positions, their skills, and performance on board. His input would have an impact on the individual men's pay, so he was diligent and fair in his remarks and assessments, especially concerning his willingness to have them serve under him again. Most of the men would leave the ship and take home leave. It was important for the Naval office to have their addresses in case they were to be called up again.

At the end of the formal exchange the Captain strode past the big warehouses and hailed a carriage to take him to Admiralty House. He both dreaded and simultaneously looked forward to his meetings there. He'd done what had been asked – to rectify the poor survival and illness statistics on the outward bound journey, and he felt proud of what he had achieved. But he was conscious that slaps on the wrist were deserved for his treatment of the bully Militia Commander before sailing, and for his sale of the government owned cannon for private usage. On the other side of the books were the premium cargo fees he had made from Simon Long, plus the regular fees for the rest of the high-value load. The cost of repairs enroute had been trivial, and the boat would be ready to sail once more in less than a month. Its newness had paid off handsomely.

While waiting to see Admiral Pennington again, sitting at a small escritoire in the ornate outer study of his office suite, the Captain quickly penned a note to his housekeeper along the lines he had described to Hutch, and paid a young messenger to deliver it forthwith. The huge oak doors flew open and the Admiral himself came striding forward, abandoning protocol by not sending his assistant out. He wasn't nearly as tall as the Captain but his handshake was as firm and sincere, and he almost bellowed, his smile and enthusiasm clearly obvious, "Welcome back, Captain Fielding. You are a pride to the Navy. Congratulations on a superb round trip. It is good to see you again. Come on in by the fire and we'll have tea..."

In an attempt to soften the reprimand he knew he was due, the Captain described all the special items he had personally collected and bought with help from his housekeeper, and how well they had been received on the outward bound trip. He followed his tale up with a suggestion that the Admiralty Lords consider a similar expenditure on future trips.

"Excellent suggestion.   Very admirable.   You are to be commended for taking the initiative to use your own savings for the purpose. I'll happily take this up with the Council when we next meet."

"Thank you, Admiral.   But I'm sure you know that not everything I did was positive. I'd like to tell my side of the story as to why I banished the Militia Commander from my ship."

"Hold it, Captain. We heard about the incident two days after you left port. We wondered what really could have transpired, as the Commander's tale that was passed to us by his superiors was incredibly complicated and confused. And then a week after you had left Portsmouth Dr. Jamieson came forward voluntarily from Portsmouth, probably suspecting your action would be viewed somewhat unfavorably. He gave us a highly detailed version of the incident, which we had no difficulty believing. In the end, frankly, there was strong support for your judgment and action. You acted in favor of the prisoners, and that was part of the charge we had assigned to you. The Council unanimously supported your behavior and I was the one who had the pleasure of going back to the bully's superiors and giving them an alternate view of what happened. I volunteered the presence of the doctor to interview if they so wished, along with seamen on your return. They declined. I know we'll insist on a different caliber of Militia leader for future trips."

Dipping his head conspiratorially and reducing his voice to a whisper, he added, "While I wouldn't repeat this officially, several of the Lords chuckled at your boldness. That doesn't happen often, believe me."

The Captain described the outward bound trip in summary form, elaborating on the extra value of picking up fresh supplies in Cape Town, and his need to leave one seaman behind there. He talked about the loss of the baby boy, offset by the joy of the little girl's arrival later, and the requests to perform several marriages before arriving in Sydney.

He gave his impression of Sydney and his view of the general state of affairs, being careful not to criticize officials but to point out the difficulties under which they worked. To the Admiral's question, "Would you take another load of convicts there again?" he calmly answered 'yes.'

"It was an adventure Sir, with thrills and challenges of the highest order. Yes, I'd do it again. Will that be an option, Sir?"

"Based on your performance, I think the Lords desperately want you to go again, but first to share your learnings with them in order to adjust the guidelines for other Captains."

The Captain recapped his negotiations for cargo to bring back home, the Admiral fully hearing how he had outwitted Mr. Long and the extra sized purse he had garnered.

"In recognition of your splendid work with the prisoners outbound, Captain Fielding, and the extraordinary level of revenue you've brought back to the coffers of government, I have no doubt there will be a significant bonus that more than doubles your stipend. You've become a symbol of what the Navy should be in this transportation business. We hold you in high esteem. The Lords have asked me to pass on their thanks. In fact, several will be waiting in the drawing room by now, anxious to meet you. Come."

"Thank you, Sir. This is most generous of you. But I think you may want a little back to replace a cannon that was lost in non-government service."

"Did you say a cannon was lost overboard through a freak wave breaking the railing near its hold-down position at the stern, Mr. Fielding? I'm sure that's something that can be readily replaced. I mean we are at war and the cannons and their shot are being manufactured in hundreds. Don't worry about it. Now do come on before the best dry sherry has been fully depleted. This way."

Chapter 26

Mrs. Hutchinson twisted her hands and wrists together for the tenth time in as many minutes, as she paced up and down the hallway. Good heavens, she thought yet again. The Captain will be home in two days! It was only ten months since he left. He thought he'd be gone closer to a full year. Must really have had very favourable winds. His letter from Sydney had arrived only three weeks before. And now he was back here already. What to do next?

She remembered an old rule of thumb. When emotions flow, make a list to help create order and logic. In the dining room she pulled out a drawer and retrieved paper and pencil. Sitting at the table she hastily scribbled items as they occurred to her – clean extra bedroom, clean Captain's room, wash bedclothes both rooms, dust both rooms, open windows, check Captain's clothes are pressed, clean stairs, check outdoor privy, buy extra fruit and vegetables, chicken and beef, make apple pie in morning of day after tomorrow, fresh milk that morning, check tea and sugar – enough? Eggs. Chimney sweep tomorrow, more coal? On and on it went. And though in the end it filled the whole page, she then put a small star beside all the items that could wait until the day after tomorrow – especially foodstuffs.

It helped to have a comprehensive list even though she knew she'd add to it as time progressed. 'Wine' she suddenly thought. Make sure to decant late afternoon two days hence. Adding to the list already. Star applied alongside. Placing the list in clear view on the kitchen table, she headed upstairs to check the narrow alcove they had had closed in and which they now called a third bedroom. The uppermost thought in her mind was that the guest must be made as comfortable as possible.

With the easing of tension throughout her body and a sense of being in control returning, she realized that it would actually be good to have the master home. Ten or twelve months – it didn't matter that much. It was a long time in either case, and now he was back. She smiled.

Flowers to brighten up the place. Another addition for the list downstairs. She hoped she'd remember.

If only she could have witnessed the scene at Admiralty House.   It was as if the Lords had been waiting for a significant occasion to have an impromptu party.   Their demeanor was a long way from that shown at tedious council meetings. The hubbub was as grand as if another war victory had just been announced.   Glasses clinked, cigar smoke circled under the ceiling, and conversation was upbeat and noisy.   As soon as the huge wooden doors from the hall opened, however, a hush gradually descended.   When it reached a sufficiently low level Admiral Pennington raised his voice and declared simply, "Gentlemen, I give you Captain Fielding!"

The members spontaneously cheered and for those with hands free there was a concomitant loud clapping. Several men stepped forward with extended arms for congratulatory handshakes.   Others clasped him on the shoulder, one pressed a drink in his left hand. For the next hour he was never alone, accosted by groups and alternately, one on one by the top men in the Navy. The Captain was somewhat overwhelmed, but pleased with the straightforward, open responses.　No condescending comments, no veiled innuendos. He was flushed with the honest warmth of recognition and unconditional thanks. His father would have been very proud.

Overnight he returned to the ship, from which more than half the cargo had been unloaded. Tomorrow he'd be back at Admiralty House for further de-briefing in greater detail, but he had promised Edward and the remaining crew to be back mid-afternoon.　He anticipated returning with information on what the Navy wanted to do with the vessel. Their decision would have an impact on whether he could let the remaining crew go or whether they'd have to help him move the ship to another set of docks immediately. Given how busy the commercial docks were, he suspected they may have to return down the Thames to Gravesend.

True to his word, by 3:30 pm he strode up the loading gangway and assembled the remaining crew. "We're headed off to Gravesend, gentlemen, as soon as we get a pilot. You will all receive extra pay, and transportation back to Admiralty House has been arranged for you. You'll be able to leave the ship the minute she is docked. Mr. Hutchinson and I will stay overnight and meet the carpenters and other officials in the morning. I know you'd like to head home right now, but I need a few more hours commitment. I thank you for your indulgence."

Exiting the Western dock required a number of cautious and slow maneuvers, but they proceeded east down the Thames without incident and were berthed by 8pm. The failing light of dusk was still in the lower sky as the Captain shook hands with each of the men disembarking, glad to be released from duty at last. Most committed to serving again, appreciating the Captain's fairness of treatment and his sailing mastery.

Edward and the Captain found dinner at a dockside pub, where they discussed how they would surprise Edward's mother on the morrow.   Edward was especially looking forward to her reaction to the gloves he had brought her. When the artisan who had crafted the gloves heard Edward's story he created a small addition. Tied with thread to the soft cuff of the left glove and hidden inside was a two inch square piece of leather on which the words 'With love from your son Edward' had been punched in tiny holes.

Edward thought that would be a surprising but nice way for his mother to learn who the Captain's companion really was. He'd save the scarves and boomerang for a later occasion.

Chapter 27

Mrs. Hutchinson headed for the markets first thing in the morning. Her strides along the cobblestone streets were strong and purposeful, her mind excitedly anticipating the day ahead. Her conversations with the stall vendors were more animated than usual and her smile was contagious. She bought peas, potatoes, and carrots, and a selection of hand-picked apples, oranges and pears. Brown eggs were carefully added to the purchases. At the meat section a plucked chicken and a dozen lamb chops went into the shopping bag, which was now reaching the limits of its capacity. She decided to splurge and get a cab home, so she made one last detour and bought three bunches of newly picked flowers. Oh yes, this was going to be an enjoyable day.

Saving herself from another walk later in the morning she had the driver stop at her favorite bakery, and picked up a variety of freshly made loaves and buns. She planned to make pound cake to augment the offerings, and for the Captain's late afternoon arrival there would be a delicious Devonshire tea served and eaten in the way the ancients had done since time immemorial. Scones split in two, each half covered with clotted cream, and strawberry jam on top. She loved baking rich fluffy scones.

The house shone from top to bottom as a result of intense spring cleaning, and the flowers added a colorful touch in the dining room, hall and kitchen. The kitchen table cloth had been washed and ironed and looked as good as the day it had been bought. The morning's baking efforts helped time race by until, with a slice of bread comprising lunch, Anne made a cream of chicken soup as her last major preparation for the Captain's arrival.

Ten months since he'd left! Ten months she'd worried about him on the high seas, as he navigated totally isolated and potentially dangerous parts of the new world.   His letters, sparse in detail as they were, provided soul-easing relief. Each one brought tears to her eyes as she thought of her 'gentle giant' writing to let her know he was all right.   There was no one in the world she cared more for, and often she wondered what she would do if, heaven forbid, he never came home again. The notion of living without him being present brought on miserable debilitating thoughts. She realized her love came from deep within, different from the love she'd once experienced with her new husband, but in some ways stronger and more rewarding. She hoped she'd be able to restrain herself in the presence of whoever was arriving with him, as she knew her first instinct would be to smother him with the pent-up love and relief she was feeling. A small shiver passed through her frame as she looked out the window for the umpteenth time willing him to magically appear once again.

As the grandfather clock in the dining room struck 3 pm she gathered the ingredients for afternoon tea and placed them on the lowest shelf behind the main kitchen cupboard door. She filled the kettle and headed upstairs to her room where she changed into her favorite dress that had been laid out across the quilted bedspread. She was not surprised to find herself shaking a little with a small line of perspiration forming around her neck. She wiped it off and told herself, 'Relax, you look fine. Just keep smiling.'

The clamor of a coachman's shouts to his horse and its insistent neighing and snorting right outside the front door was the signal she'd been waiting for. Through the kitchen window she saw the Captain and his friend alight and the coachman start handing down the Captain's trunks. She whipped off her apron and rushed to open the front door. The Captain turned and smiled as she came racing up to hug him.   Arms around his neck, her ample bosom pressed against his abdomen, she cried into his waistcoat. "It is so good to see you Captain. Welcome home. I've been waiting so long."

"Mrs. Hutch, it's wonderful to see you too, and so good to be home at last.   Now, let me introduce my friend Edward. He's been away 8 years, and anxious to learn about what's changed in the years he's been gone."

"Well, young man, it's a pleasure to meet you. I bid you welcome. Any friend of the Captain is welcome here. You come on in and make yourself right at home. I hope you like Devonshire Tea. I'll go and put the kettle on and make the scones while you help bring the luggage inside."

With that she turned and headed back across the pavement. Just before entering the house something made her stop and turn back. She found Edward looking straight at her and grinning from ear to ear.

She paused, breathed out a huge sigh and said, "You know Mister, especially with that grin on your face, you certainly do have a familiar look about you...."

****

Illustration

Page 62, Courtesy Boston Museum of Fine Arts

A Heptagonal Bag, French, about 1800. Old rose moiré silk panels on steel cockade frame. Cut steel rosettes at rivets. Steel turn-key closure. White ribbon on steel rings. White silk lining.

Author's Biography

Having a convict ancestor, Warren has extensively researched the history of convict times, writing about the trials, tribulations, and trepidation faced by normal English citizens who were trapped into poverty and crime, convicted, and sent to the Antipodes. In general they experienced terrible prison conditions in old ships crossing turbulent oceans, arriving in an alien land totally mismanaged by authorities.

This story is about one specific voyage, written from the perspective of the captain who was responsible for the healthy delivery of his human cargo. It details the arrangements and conditions prisoners endured between an English embarkation port and their destination at Sydney Cove. Most convicts had never been to sea and the new experience was one of tremendous doubt, terror, and apprehension. In the middle of the vast Atlantic and Indian Oceans, with no land in sight for months, and fearsome storms scaring them witless. they had nothing to cling to except faith in the captain's seamanship and the seaworthiness of the vessel in which they were cocooned.

Many ships never made it all the way; some of their wrecks being found on rugged South African coastlines, with as many never being heard of again. Captains and crews needed to be braver than their passengers. Or at least appear so.

In the diary of one who made it:

"Those who go to sea should have neither nose nor ears, for booms and bulk-heads will creak and provisions emanate odours pas haut-a–fait agreeable. A sailor does not live in the present but in satisfaction and anticipation. Hence the frequent 'How soon shall we reach such a place? 'and the most important topic of conversation is the Wind. To conclude this greatest pleasure of a voyage is the end of it, and I may venture to affirm that the cry of 'Land!' was never yet heard without joy, even by one of so loving a disposition that he would go to sea the next day again."

[Quote taken from "Journal of a Voyage from ENGLAND to SYDNEY,   NEW SOUTH WALES, by Eliza Taylor, 1835", Australian National Maritime Museum, Sydney, Australia.]